Runaround

Helen Hemphill

FRONT STREET
Asheville, North Carolina

for Jo and Sherry

Copyright © 2007 by Helen Hemphill
All rights reserved
Printed in China
Designed by Helen Robinson
First edition
Second printing

Library of Congress Cataloging-in-Publication Data
Hemphill, Helen.
Runaround / by Helen Hemphill.
p. cm.
Summary: In Kentucky in the 1960s, partly as revenge against her older sister for
publicly embarrassing her, eleven-year-old Sassy decides to make the handsomest
boy in the neighborhood her boyfriend, but first she has to find out what
makes a boy like a girl, and how to know when he does.
ISBN-13: 978-1-932425-83-3 (hardcover : alk. paper)
[1. Sisters—Fiction. 2. Love—Fiction. 3. Family life—Kentucky—Fiction.
4. Single-parent families—Fiction. 5. Kentucky—History—20th century—Fiction.] I. Title.
PZ7.H3774487Run 2007
[Fic]—dc22
2006020310

Front Street
An Imprint of Boyds Mills Press, Inc.
815 Church Street
Honesdale, Pennsylvania 18431

RUNAROUND

I NEED TO KNOW HOW TO GET A BOYFRIEND, SO A CERTAIN **SOMEONE** WILL LIKE ME AND MAKE MY OLDER SISTER SICK WITH JEALOUSY. PLEASE WRITE BACK QUICK WITH SPECIFIC INSTRUCTIONS. DON'T LEAVE ANYTHING OUT.

"I ain't telling you nothing about the birds and bees." Miss Dallas pitched watery ice cubes from her glass into the dry August dirt. "I'm not your mama."

"But I ain't got a mama," Sassy said. "How am I going to ask my mama when I ain't got one?" She wet her finger and rubbed the chigger bites along the backs of her legs. "Besides, I never said one word about birds and bees. You made that up."

Sassy sat with Miss Dallas on the kitchen porch step, looking out over a patch of tobacco and a thirsty vegetable garden. A sprinkler fanned a thin column of water through the late-summer tomatoes, while the sun hovered against a low line of trees.

"Then why all the questions about romance?" Miss Dallas asked. "You in love?"

"No!"

"So you're just curious all of a sudden?"

"Maybe."

A put-on innocence sparked in Miss Dallas's

eyes. "Well, I don't know anything about romance myself," she said. "Not a thing." She plucked a fine gray hair from the widow's peak on her forehead.

Sassy blinked a deadpan glare. How *could* Miss Dallas know anything? She hadn't even read one story in the *Love Confessions* magazines that Sassy had sneaked home from Methodist church camp. Sassy had read every single *Love Confessions* from cover to cover. But the more she read, the more questions came.

"Why don't you ask your daddy?" Miss Dallas said.

"I can't ask Daddy. It's too personal." Sassy's face warmed up hot, even in the late afternoon shade. "I ain't asking a boy."

"Well, what exactly do you want to know, anyhow?"

Sassy pushed a string of dirty hair behind her ear and picked at her toenail.

"You want to know how to make a baby?" Miss Dallas nudged Sassy's shoulder.

"No!" Sassy already knew about that from girls' health class. Last year, they had even showed a filmstrip of a baby being born, all bloody and bawling. It was nasty-looking.

"Well, what then?"

"Nothing."

"So you been after me all afternoon about nothing?"

"Not nothing," Sassy said. "I ain't at liberty to give you details, that's all. It's none of your beeswax."

"Well, if it's not my business, then I'll just keep my little old mouth shut." Miss Dallas pursed her lips and mimed turning a key with her fingers.

Sometimes Sassy wanted to pinch Miss Dallas's arm until a big blue whelp raised up, but Daddy would have her hide if she did. So she stuck out her tongue instead.

"I'll cut that off!"

"Daddy'll take the belt after you!" But Sassy knew he'd do no

such thing. It wasn't easy finding someone to baby-sit two girls like Sassy and her older sister, Lula. At least that's what Daddy always said. Probably 'cause Lula was so two-faced and mean.

Sassy raked her dark hair to the back of her neck. She looked straight down at the worn wood of the step and spoke real quiet. "I want to know about boys," she said. "How does a girl know if a boy likes her? Really likes her—boyfriend–girlfriend like?"

Miss Dallas laughed deep down in her throat. "Well, don't be asking your daddy, then."

"Why not?"

"'Cause he'll lock you in your room until you're eighteen. You're not old enough to have a boyfriend."

"I'm almost twelve!"

"Twelve? You might as well go on and get married. Another year and you'll be an old maid!" Miss Dallas got up and squeezed the water hose until the sprinkler slowed to a wet dribble.

"It's not funny!"

"You reading those romance magazines again?"

"So?"

"Love's not some made-up fairy tale, Sassy."

"I thought you didn't know anything about romance!"

"I know that much. I wouldn't say a word to your daddy if I was you."

"I ain't got a boyfriend!"

"And I'm sure you're telling the whole truth and nothing but the truth." Miss Dallas pulled the sprinkler along the tomato plants, then released the hose. Water sprayed out into the air, sending a mist that settled on Sassy's face and legs.

Sassy huffed out a sigh and made a show of wiping her eyes. "If you was any kind of baby-sitter, you would tell me about boys."

Miss Dallas adjusted the sprinkler once more. "I guess I'm just a failure, then."

"I guess you are."

Talking to Miss Dallas had been a big waste of time, but Sassy had never gotten a reply from the romance editor of *Love Confessions*, even though she had written more than a week ago. There wasn't a soul she could trust in the whole town of Falls of Rough—maybe the whole state of Kentucky.

"You going to start pestering Lula now?"

"I ain't asking Lula nothing."

"She's got a boyfriend or two, I reckon," Miss Dallas said.

"She thinks every boy's her boyfriend."

"They don't seem to mind none." Miss Dallas watched the sprinkler. She might have been pretty once, but Sassy hadn't seen more than a handful of smiles from the woman in all the years she'd been with the girls. She was no substitute for Mama. Mama always smiled like a dazzling movie star in every single one of her pictures in the photo album. She was young and beautiful. Sassy wished like crazy she could remember just one of Mama's smiles in person. But it was too long ago.

Sassy fidgeted with indecision. "Well, what if I *did* ask Daddy?" she said. "He knows everything about being sweethearts. He adored my mama more than anything on this earth. He told me that hisself."

"I'm sure he's a bona fide expert," Miss Dallas said. "Go ahead and ask him." Miss Dallas picked up her glass and scraped the mud from the soles of her loafers along the edge of the back porch step.

Sassy stood up and dusted off the seat of her shorts. She was done talking.

"I want you to go to the Cheap Cash before supper," Miss Dallas said. "We need a loaf of bread and some milk for in the morning. If you hurry up, you might have time to ask your daddy before Lula starts prancing around to get his attention. He'll be home directly."

Sassy opened the screen door wide. "I never said I was going to ask him."

"Well, excuse me," Miss Dallas said. "But while you're wrestling with your decision, go on to the store. I got to start supper."

"Don't think I'm going to tell you what Daddy says." Sassy fished her shoes from the window ledge on the back porch. "You'll have to make sense of boyfriends all on your own."

"Hwhoo!" Miss Dallas said. "There's not a man in the world I'd have."

"Well, that's good. I bet no man would want you, ornery as you are." Sassy snapped the grocery list from Miss Dallas's hand and let the screen door slam against the house.

Maybe she would ask Daddy. But she wouldn't say a word about Boon. What Daddy didn't know wouldn't hurt him.

2

Sassy's first kiss happened the second week of church camp. For once in a blue moon, Lula had been agreeable and let Sassy sneak out with the older girls to the senior boys' cabin to play spin the bottle.

"Now hush, everybody, so I can explain the rules." Lula tossed her long gold ponytail to the side of her shoulder. Lula Willis Thompkins, with clear blue eyes, was magazine pretty, just like Mama. But pretty is as pretty does, and Lula had been nothing but a wicked-witch sister all summer. It seemed as if everything and everybody irritated her.

"I'll start off." Lula spun the bottle, but it wobbled toward Reeves Hanvey, stopping on him after he stuck his foot in its path. Hollers of protest filled the cabin.

"It was an accident!" Reeves crossed his heart, but the other boys knew better. Reeves was just one in a long line of Lula's hopeful boyfriends.

"Reeves, we have to play fair. I'm not going

A GIRL DOESN'T EVER FORGET HER FIRST KISS. IT'S A GHOST THAT HAUNTS ALL THE OTHER KISSES OF HER LIFE.

to kiss you at all." Lula grinned until Reeves's face flushed the shade of a ripe tomato. "But you have to spin the bottle and kiss the first girl it lands on," Lula said. "Then *that* girl spins the bottle and kisses a boy, and so on, and so on. Everybody has to kiss right out here in the middle of the circle, so, Reeves, play nice, now." Lula's eyes teased, and she smoothed her hair. "Y'all ready?"

Anxious laughter swept through the room as Lula handed the Coca-Cola bottle to Reeves. Sassy chewed on the end of her hair and tried not to look.

The bottle spun in a slow loop and finally stopped in an empty space between Sassy and another boy. Reeves flicked the neck of the bottle with his fingernail until it nudged over on Sassy. Did Reeves want to kiss her? Excited giggles tittered around the circle.

A warm blush rushed up Sassy's face. Reeves was only half cute, with a pimply chin and an oversize nose. But his daddy owned most of the tobacco farmland from Falls of Rough to the Kentucky border, and that gave him a kind of irresistible charm.

"Okay, Sassy, you're in the circle!" Lula said. "Kiss her good, Reeves."

"Then do I get to kiss you?" Reeves asked.

Lula didn't smile, but her voice was all sweetie sweet. "Not now!"

Sassy stood up in the middle of the room, pulled her shirt straight, and held her hand over her mouth. She burped up the faint taste of a mustard hot dog. Reeves paused in front of her. Did he know it was her first kiss?

Sassy tilted her chin to keep her nose from bumping right into his and held her breath just like she had read in *Love Confessions*. Her knees wobbled. She closed her eyes and did her best to pucker her lips in a pout worthy of a Hollywood movie close-up. Someone sniggered.

Then, it was over.

Reeves pecked at her lips so fast, Sassy wasn't sure he had kissed her at all. She opened her eyes, but Reeves was already sitting down. He had left her standing by herself.

"Now what kind of kiss was that?" Lula asked. "You ever kiss a girl before?" The boys all howled and whistled, and the girls whispered behind their hands.

"She kisses worse than a suckerfish," Reeves announced to the whole cabin. "I ain't kissing no fish lips."

Every jeering eye in the cabin burned into Sassy. Air stuck in her throat. She stared at Lula to do something. To tell Reeves to hush. To shut up. To leave Sassy alone. But Lula laughed. Lula's ponytail bobbed up and down when Reeves sucked in his cheeks and made a fish face. She held her sides and snorted out giggles— making fun of her own sister. Sassy stared at Lula's ponytail and Reeves's lips until an explosion spewed out of her.

"I'll bust your mouth wide open if you say that again!" Sassy yelled.

"Fish Lips!" Reeves kept at it.

"Shut your trap!"

"Fish Lips!" Reeves eyed the door.

Sassy started after him, and Reeves hightailed it out through the porch screen. Sassy dove for his ankle, caught his hairy leg, and buried her fingers deep into his calf muscle. Reeves screamed.

"Say one more word and you're going to need some stitches in that pimply face!" Sassy hollered. Reeves kicked at her, and Coca-Cola bottles went flying.

Then, Sassy aimed a right hook toward Reeves and caught his nose in a solid thud. Blood poured out like a water spigot.

"Goll darn it! Get her off me!" he yelled.

One of Lula's boyfriends dragged Sassy away from Reeves,

and the coward escaped into the dark

"You better run, you scaredy-cat liar!" Sassy squirmed against her pinned arms. "I'll bust your lip, and you can kiss my butt!"

Everybody laughed like it was some *I Love Lucy* episode. Three cabins down, a counselor, jarred out of a dead sleep from the noise of the ruckus, tattled to the camp administrator, and within ten minutes the girls were marched back to their cabins. Every one of them was cited with a Christian values violation.

"Remember jokes?" Lula lashed out on the trudge back to the girls' cabin. "We were having fun tonight. Couldn't you tell that Reeves was just teasing you? You couldn't go along and laugh it off—oh, no! You and your temper! This is your fault."

The next night, a dried spotted suckerfish ended up in Sassy's bunk. *A joke, my foot*, Sassy thought. The next morning, she got into a shouting match with Lula, after Lula sided with Reeves and the whole group of would-be boyfriends, calling Sassy a little hellion. Her own sister turned traitor. Daddy had to come get Sassy from camp a week early.

Reeves had ruined Sassy's first kiss, and her sister had laughed. Sassy wasn't about to forgive Lula. There would be no making up. No sisterly love. No bygones. Nothing would fix things but good, honest revenge.

The plan was Boon. Boon Hoyt Chisholm was no ordinary boy. He was almost a year older than Lula and drop-dead gorgeous. All Sassy needed was for Boon to fall head over heels for her, then she could flaunt the cutest boyfriend in the world right under her sister's nose. Boon would make Reeves seem like a hand-me-down. And wouldn't that just send Lula into a green-eyed jealous fit?

Now, the late afternoon sun spotlighted shadows on the steps of the Cheap Cash. The store was empty except for Mr. Frankie, who stood at the counter reading the newspaper.

"Afternoon," he said, but he never looked up. Mr. Frankie was a tall, pale man with a bony face and watery green eyes. His grand-daddy had opened the store during the Depression, but everyone knew nothing at the Cheap Cash was cheap. Now Mr. Frankie was old enough to be a granddaddy himself, but he wasn't married. He was an old maid of a man, cranky and cantankerous.

"Anything interesting in the paper?" Sassy asked.

Mr. Frankie stretched his neck against the starched collar of his shirt. He turned the page of the paper. "Sugar! The Yanks whipped the White Sox 7–3," he said. "Mickey Mantle switch-hit two home runs—beats all I've ever seen." Mr. Frankie looked up.

Sassy leaned over and scanned the advertisements. "Is *A Hard Day's Night* on at the Leitchfield picture show? It just came out yesterday."

"I guess you'll need to buy the paper and find out," Mr. Frankie said. He folded the newspaper until it was all neat, ready to be sold. "I wouldn't pay a nickel to see those long-haired girls."

Sassy didn't want to argue with Mr. Frankie about The Beatles, especially when his radio was always tuned to hillbilly music on The Grand Ole Opry. "Miss Dallas gave me a list." Sassy handed him a small square of white notebook paper.

"Hold on. Hold on." Mr. Frankie eyed the list and then pulled at his collar. "Don't have my new grocery stock out yet," he said. "Got to get the coffee from the storeroom." He headed toward the back. "We ordered some new cherry syrup that tastes mighty good in Coca-Cola, if you're interested."

"Maybe," Sassy said. "But I didn't bring my baby-sitting money."

"I'll let you put it on your daddy's account," Mr. Frankie called to her. "Imagine he's good for it."

The Cheap Cash was the only grocery from Falls of Rough

to Caneyville that allowed credit. Sassy listened to Mr. Frankie scrape crates along the floor. "Sugar! I don't know why Miss Dallas dotes so much on Maryland Club Coffee. ..." But his voice got lost in the whine of the store's fluorescent lights.

Sassy thumbed through the magazine rack, but the issue of *Love Confessions* was the same one she already had under her pillow.

"New magazines won't be here until in the morning."

Sassy jumped a little at the sound of Mr. Frankie's voice. "Just looking," she said.

"You want those crazy Beatle fan magazines, young lady?" Mr. Frankie carried a Tall Boy Soup box and a two-pound-size coffee can.

"No, sir," Sassy answered.

"I'd like to give those boys a crew cut. You seen them on TV?"

Everyone alive on the planet Earth had seen The Beatles on *Ed Sullivan*; didn't Mr. Frankie know that? "Just looking for the new issue of *Love Confessions*," Sassy said.

"Humph." Mr. Frankie's eyes lingered on her. "Your daddy let you read that junk?" He didn't wait for an answer. "Got to get the sweet milk out of the shed cooler. How 'bout that cherry Coke?"

"Sure," Sassy said. "I had one at the movie show in Leitchfield." But Mr. Frankie was already behind the meat counter headed outside to the shed.

Sassy sat down at the soda fountain and let her feet dangle to the floor.

She spun around on the stool.

Maybe Boon would take her to see *A Hard Day's Night*. Since coming home from Methodist church camp ten days ago, Sassy had seen Boon twice at the Cheap Cash. Once, he tipped his hat at her when he was leaving. Then, the next time, he had smiled at her. Right to her face. That easy smile with the perfect white teeth—the color of fine sugar.

Sassy spun around on the stool again. But where was Boon now? This very minute?

If he was her flame in *Love Confessions*, he would walk right in the door, take her into his arms, and tell her he loved her and couldn't live one more second without her. It could happen—but she had to talk to him first. Boon attended Caneyville Graded School with Lula and Sassy, but Sassy had never actually spoken to him. Neither had Lula, as far as Sassy knew.

The whole Chisholm clan was off limits to the girls. Miss Dallas said that Mrs. Chisholm was real good at *getting* married and not so good at *staying* married. Rumor in town was that husband number four had been run off the Chisholm place shortly after Memorial Day with nothing but his underwear and a bottle of Jack Daniels, and now Mrs. Chisholm was on the prowl for lucky number five.

Fifteen years ago, Boon's daddy had been dragged from the altar by his overbearing mama. The Chisholms changed their wild pregnant daughter's name from *Miss* to *Mrs.*, and the would-be husband was never mentioned again. No one in town begrudged Boon's illegitimacy exactly, but there wasn't a daddy in the county who wanted his daughter dating Boon, either. Boon was Maybelle Chisholm's boy, and he couldn't fall far enough away from that tree. Not that the daughters cared one bit.

Sassy twisted the stool counterclockwise as far as she could, then let her hands go. Spinning like a 45 single, the whole grocery store melted into a light-headed, luminous blur. Queasy—head over heels. That's how she wanted Boon to feel about her.

Sassy spun around again, but this time, her left shoe flew from her foot just as the door rattled open. Sassy grabbed the counter and stopped the revolving stool up short. She held on tight and let her head settle. Cupid must have been working overtime. There was Boon—holding her shoe in his hand like Prince Charming.

3

Boon touched the brim of his grown-up man's hat. Even with his worn, rumpled shirt, he looked like a living doll. "Hey, Sassy," he said. "You lose something?" His eyes smiled the color of Miss Dallas's summer hydrangeas—violet blue. Nobody Sassy had ever seen had eyes that color, except maybe Elizabeth Taylor in *National Velvet*.

"Hey," she said. "I guess it got away from me."

"Put your foot up here," Boon said. He patted his knee.

Sassy thought she might stop breathing. She raised her foot and Boon guided it to his knee, then placed the worn yellow rubber strip of her sandal between her toes. Dirt had collected under her toenails, but Boon didn't seem to notice.

"There you go," he said. "Another glass slipper returned safe and sound." Boon made a little bow and grinned. "Didn't I see you the other day?" he asked. "We got to quit meeting like this. I bet they're gossiping all over town about us."

HE WALKED IN, AND THE WORLD TILTED ON ITS SIDE. THE UNIVERSE EXPANDED INTO A FULL BREATH OF SPRING, AND IT WAS **LOVE** AT FIRST SIGHT.

Sassy smiled.

He leaned forward and spoke low, like he was telling a secret. "You weren't following me, were you?"

"How could I follow you? I was already here," Sassy said.

"But you're sure you weren't following me? Checking up on my whereabouts?" Boon cocked his head as if he knew the answer.

Sassy's mouth flattened into a stern line. "No!"

"You sure?" he said.

"Sure," she said. "Somebody looking for you?"

"Think so? I don't know—might be." Boon winked at her, then looked through her, toward the back of the store. "Mr. Frankie here?" Boon patted his shirt pocket. "I have a little business to transact."

"He's out at the shed getting me some milk from the cooler," Sassy said. "Probably won't be long."

"I'll wait with you," Boon said. He sat next to her, and Sassy breathed in Boon's smell, something akin to sweat and soap. A raw shiver ran along her shoulder blades and arms, but it wasn't cold in the room.

Boon laid his hat on the counter. His black hair crowded his collar. "How y'all been?" he said. "Don't think I've seen your daddy in a month, and I haven't laid eyes on Lula all summer. Y'all hiding her in the cellar?"

"Lula's here. I mean, she's at home kissing some Elvis picture, I guess," Sassy said. "She got back from church camp Thursday. Daddy went and got her. Can you believe school starts in less than a month?" Sassy jiggled her foot the whole time she talked.

"Time flies, don't it?" Boon's voice was slow and effortless.

"And Daddy's hardly ever at the house. Worried silly about that smoking report from the surgeon general fella," Sassy continued. "Miss Dallas says the government can't keep people from growing tobacco, and that surgeon is just trying to scare everybody. That's what Daddy says, too. Cigarettes can't turn your lungs black. I don't care what …"

Boon laughed out loud and rubbed his hand through his hair.

Sassy shut up. Why did she have to run on about tobacco? "That's what they said. …" Her voice got small and shaky. "It was on Walter Cronkite." She frowned hard. How in Hades did a girl ever learn to flirt?

"Now don't get all huffy and sour-faced like that," Boon said. "You're almost pretty if you don't get to looking like you ate too many Sweet Tarts."

Sassy spun her stool away from Boon. Sour-faced? The warm air of the store circled around Sassy. She wished more than anything she was beautiful, but Lula was the pretty girl in the family. In *Love Confessions*, a girl might start crying her eyes out about now.

The back door opened for a minute. "Hello?" Boon called. "Mr. Frankie?" There was no answer. Boon shrugged and drummed his fingers along the counter. An awkward silence settled in.

Sassy searched her brain for some sliver of news that would make her funny or fascinating to Boon. If only she could be a mind reader for a minute. What was Boon thinking?

Sassy picked at some old nail polish on her fingernail. One of Lula's friends had painted Sassy's nails at church camp, but now the polish was chipped and worn. She chewed on a dry cuticle, then looked up. Boon's glance caught her eye, and he grinned that effortless, blinding smile.

Sassy said the first thing that popped into her head. "Boon, anybody ever tell you that you got real white teeth? They're nice. You must brush them all the time."

Boon looked puzzled. "Not all the time," he said.

His eyes skirted around her face. Did he think she was pretty, even a little bit?

"People around here don't have nice teeth much," Sassy said.

"I never thought about it," he said. "Wonder why that is?"

"I don't know." Again, Sassy sat silent, disappointed in herself. Not once in *Love Confessions* did girlfriends and boyfriends ever talk about brushing their teeth.

Mr. Frankie came inside carrying a crate of milk cartons.

"Afternoon, sir," Boon said. "Mama asked me to do some bill paying, and I got a list of things, too—wrote on the envelope for you. Powdered milk for the baby, a couple of those Chef Boyardee box pizzas, and some clothes-washing soap." Boon slid the envelope across the counter.

Mr. Frankie didn't answer Boon. "You up for that cherry Coke, Sassy?" he asked.

"Can I take a paper cup? Miss Dallas told me not to dillydally too long." Sassy chewed on her lip to bring up its rosy color, just like it said to do in the *Love Confessions* beauty column. Maybe she could stay a minute longer.

Mr. Frankie filled a paper cup with ice and looked back at Boon. "I thought your mother was coming by to see me about the bill."

"She never said."

Mr. Frankie dried his hands and opened the envelope. "Well, I can't give you any more credit."

"I just gave you a payment."

"Not enough here to buy the groceries, much less what y'all owe."

"Well, if you didn't charge so much for everything ..."

Mr. Frankie counted out the odd dollar bills and change from Boon's envelope and tidied the cash drawer. "Your mother better be going on assistance," he said. "Washington's handing out those new Food Stamps right and left. Somebody might as well start paying to feed those kids."

Sassy ran her thumb along the edge of the counter. She couldn't look at Boon anymore.

"Charity's run out," Mr. Frankie said. He set the cherry Coke in front of Sassy and ripped a charge slip from his book. "Give this receipt to Miss Dallas."

Boon never moved, but his voice seemed strained. "I need those groceries," he said.

"You got the money?" Mr. Frankie glared hard at him. "No money. No groceries."

Sassy looked down at the floor.

Boon cracked his knuckles and laughed. "Now Mr. Frankie, you don't want to miss some good business here, sir. I know you don't. Six kids eat a lot of groceries. Mama's catching things up, and I know she'll come settle with you. No need to be a fuss-budget about all this. Everything will work out."

The old man leaned over the counter. "Maybe you didn't hear me, Boon. No cash. No groceries. Now go on home and tell your mama like I told you to."

But Boon didn't move. Sassy couldn't even tell if he was breathing. His jaw set hard like one of those boxers Daddy watched on the *Friday Night Fights*. Sassy got scared.

"I'll buy them," she blurted out. "Put the groceries on Daddy's ticket. I got baby-sitting money to pay him back."

Mr. Frankie and Boon stared at her. The drone of the fluorescent lights filled their frozen silence.

"I mean, I don't mind a bit. Happy to do it," Sassy said.

Something churned in Boon's eyes, then his smile opened up like sunshine. "Sassy, you are too good to me. I might just kiss you."

A bright happiness filled Sassy's insides. Lula might as well get out the crying towel. How could Boon not like a girl who would help him out of a jam?

4

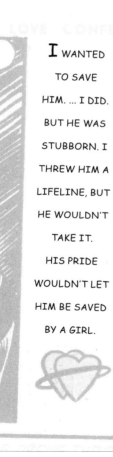

I WANTED TO SAVE HIM. ... I DID. BUT HE WAS STUBBORN. I THREW HIM A LIFELINE, BUT HE WOULDN'T TAKE IT. HIS PRIDE WOULDN'T LET HIM BE SAVED BY A GIRL.

"You're not going to buy this boy's groceries," Mr. Frankie clamped his mouth in a tight little line across his face, "because I'm not going to sell them to you."

"I got the money! You have to sell them," Sassy said.

"I don't see any cash from either one of you," Mr. Frankie said. "Now get on out of here."

"You said my account was good for it."

"I meant it's your daddy's account, young lady," Mr. Frankie said.

"I'm gonna pay Daddy back as soon as I get home," Sassy said.

Boon put his hand on Sassy's shoulder. "What kind of church-going Christian are you, Mr. Frankie? Sassy's just being a Good Samaritan. ..."

"She's being a busybody little girl," Mr. Frankie said. "Sassy, this don't concern you."

Boon slipped his arm around Sassy's waist, and she liked standing so near to him.

"You can't talk to her that way," Boon said.

Sassy nodded in agreement. "No disrespect, Mr. Frankie, but I can do whatever I want with my baby-sitting money," she said. "Daddy don't have no say over it."

"Don't smart-mouth me," Mr. Frankie said. "Now, take Miss Dallas's things and your Coke and go on home."

"Mr. Frankie, you better sell me everything on Boon's list!"

"I won't do any such thing," he said. "Go home."

"I'm just going to start screaming if you don't," she said.

"You better not! I'll run you out of here."

"I'll scream if I want to, and I can scream louder than anybody in Grayson County. Just ask Miss Dallas."

"Don't threaten me!" Mr. Frankie took the neat newspaper and rolled it into a tight baton. "Start that up, and I'll take this newspaper after you."

"You better not touch me," Sassy bragged. "My daddy would be down here whipping you all over the store. Ain't that right, Boon?"

"You know he will," Boon said. He grinned at Mr. Frankie.

"I'll take my chances," Mr. Frankie said. He swatted the newspaper in the air but missed Sassy by a mile.

"Okay, but I warned you! You're going to be sorrier than an old deaf dog." Sassy inhaled and let loose with an eyes-wide-open scream that sliced the air with the precision of a tornado siren.

Mr. Frankie jumped back at the sheer screech of the noise. "Holy sugar!" he said. "Stop that!"

Boon laughed and gigged Sassy in the side, sending off squeals of laughter that echoed off the rafters of the old building.

Mr. Frankie pounded the newspaper on the counter. "Stop that right now!"

Boon tickled Sassy again, and her wild scream-giggles started all over.

"You little hellcat! Hush that up!" Mr. Frankie's voice drowned to a dull bellow as Sassy screamed even louder. She couldn't hear a word Mr. Frankie was saying now. Instead, she could see him mouthing the words *shut up* over and over and over like a silent movie. "Shut up! Shut up!" Mr. Frankie yelled. "God Almighty, shut up!"

Sassy stopped. "You selling me the groceries?" she asked.

Boon waited for Mr. Frankie's reply.

"Not on God's green earth!" Mr. Frankie said, waving the baton of newsprint. "Get out of here before I call the sheriff. You're disturbing the peace."

Boon goosed Sassy again, and she blasted away again, shattering the quiet with all the power her lungs could muster.

"Sugar! What is wrong with you?" Mr. Frankie said. "Shut up, I said!"

Still Sassy screamed.

Mr. Frankie whacked her on the top of her head with the newspaper.

But the scream settled into an endless tortured ear-piercing that warbled only when Sassy breathed, and Sassy could hold her breath a good long time.

Finally, the old man pressed his palms into his ears and half-crouched behind the counter. "For the love of God, stop!" he said. "Just stop! I'll sell you the whole store!"

Sassy stopped in midscream.

Mr. Frankie tilted his head to test the sound. "Your daddy ought to take duct tape after that loud mouth of yours," he said.

"You made me do it. If you weren't so stingy, I wouldn't have said a peep," Sassy smarted off.

"Just keep quiet!" Mr. Frankie pulled the envelope out of the trash and gathered Boon's groceries on the counter. "Don't think I won't tell your daddy about this."

"Go right ahead. I might just tell him myself." Sassy smiled over at Boon. He winked at her, and Sassy's insides melted.

Mr. Frankie packed Boon's groceries around her own, then wrote out the ticket. "I suppose you want two cherry Cokes, too?"

"Why, yes, please," she said. Sassy sounded only a little phony using the *p* word.

Mr. Frankie slammed the pencil on the counter and poured cherry syrup into another paper cup; the Coke fizzled into the air. He set the cup on the counter next to Sassy's. "Here's your new ticket," he said. "Now get out of here. Soon as I talk to your daddy, you won't be laughing."

"Boon, would you help me carry the groceries? I need to get on home," Sassy said. Outside, the sun was almost gone in a haze of twilight.

Boon didn't speak but put on his hat and bowed low like an actor at a curtain call. He slid the box off the counter and under his arm, grinned at Sassy like they were conspirators, and then flung open the door with a full jerk.

"You'll work for me if you break that door," Mr. Frankie yelled after him. "Tell your mother she better get over here about this bill!"

Sassy tucked the ticket into her pocket and balanced the Cokes, one in each hand. Boon had already crossed the blacktop road, waiting for her. "I wouldn't be so high and mighty about your cherry Cokes," she said to Mr. Frankie. "In Leitchfield, they put in real cherries."

Juggling the full cups as best she could, Sassy ran to meet Boon. The drinks splashed over the sides, cold and sticky.

How could she be so lucky? She had come to Boon's rescue and saved the day just like one of the beautiful heroines in *Love Confessions*. She didn't need to talk to Daddy now because Boon was probably crazy grateful in love. Besides, he had to like her— she liked him.

5

HE SHOULD KISS THE GROUND I WALK ON, BUT INSTEAD HE SAYS HE LOVES HIS MOTHER MORE THAN HE DOES ME. HE'S KNOWN HER LONGER.

"You got one set of lungs, Sassy girl," Boon said. "Old Man Frankie won't be hearing good for a week." He shifted the grocery box against his shoulder and walked with Sassy toward her house.

Sassy followed him. "He deserved it for being so selfish," she said. "I felt sorry for the way he treated you."

Boon gave her a hurried look and picked up his pace.

"Daddy says Mr. Frankie is just a lonely old man, but he's stingy—that's why he don't have no friends. Who wants to be nice to a mean old Scrooge? It's not like he don't know y'all need help. Everybody in Falls of Rough knows that." Sassy had to walk fast to stay up with Boon, but the Cokes sloshed all over her legs and shoes.

"What makes you think we need help?" Boon asked.

"'Cause ya'll are poor," Sassy said. She wasn't about to tell Boon it was because he had a no-count mama. "Miss Dallas says that every baby comes in this world buck-naked, so we all got to try and make something of ourselves, but the way I see it, that's not really true. Just think about John-John and Caroline. They got boatloads of family money and their daddy was president. They were born naked, but they weren't really full-fledged, show-off naked. I mean, they came from good people, and they don't need help. ..."

The Cokes splashed onto the blacktop, reminding Sassy she was still holding them both. "Don't you want your cherry Coke?"

"I guess I don't," Boon said. "I don't *need* it."

Boon walked so fast, Sassy had to about run beside him, but she couldn't run with the Cokes. Sassy stopped and steadied the cups, then started again. "But I got it for you!"

"I don't want it!"

Sassy held the drinks out in front of her as she quickened her pace. "Boon, why are you mad? We got the groceries!"

Boon walked faster.

"Mr. Frankie acted like a horse's behind. I just wanted to help." Sassy said. Cherry Coke ran down the side of her arm and dripped from her elbow. "I didn't mean anything."

Boon shifted the box and never looked back.

"Boon! I can't run with these Cokes." Sassy eyed the liquid, jostling up the sides of the paper cups with every step, and speeded on as best she could.

Brown drops made long streaks down her hands. She was right behind Boon.

In a sudden turn, Boon swung around and stopped in front of her. Sassy ran smack into him, and the Cokes tumbled out of her hands and onto the ground, splashing her shirt and shorts.

"Dang it!" Sassy yelled. She jumped back, but a dark circle soaked the front of her cotton shirt. "This was my last clean shirt!" she said. "Now Miss Dallas will be after me about the ironing. Why did you just stop like that?"

"How did I know you were right behind me?"

"I was talking to you!" Sassy pulled the wet fabric out in front of her and fanned it away from her skin.

"Ever think you talk too much?" Boon lowered the grocery box to the ground and picked up the paper cups from the sticky mud.

Sassy fanned her blouse harder. "I didn't mind that you never said *howdy do* about me getting the groceries for you, but you sure could be a little nicer. You were all smiles at the Cheap Cash."

"So."

"I guess you didn't mind me getting in trouble with Mr. Frankie."

Boon flicked the muddy liquid into the weeds and pitched the cups into the box. "Wait just a minute," he said. "The screaming was your idea."

"I was trying to help." Sassy wiped the Coke stain with the palm of her hand.

"I didn't ask you to butt in," Boon said.

"You sure weren't getting anywhere with Mr. Frankie on your own."

"He's a stubborn jackass," Boon said. The color of Boon's eyes was almost purple now. "And I didn't need your help."

"You didn't have any money and you didn't have any credit. How exactly did you not need my help?"

Boon put up his hands and backed away. "I heard enough of this," he said. "I got things to do." He turned and walked through the weeds.

"You want your groceries, or you want me to throw them in the ditch?" Sassy yelled after Boon.

He turned around. A muscle tightened along his jaw, and he glared right at her. "I want them," he said.

Sassy handed him the clothes-washing soap without saying anything.

Boon piled the groceries in his arms. "How you going to

handle the charge ticket with your daddy?"

"I didn't plan on telling him exactly," Sassy said.

A half smile crossed Boon's face. "I appreciate that, I do."

"So you're thankful for something, then?"

"I'll pay you back as soon as I can."

"I'm not going anywhere."

"I'm poor, so it might take a while." Boon's voice had a sarcastic edge.

"Is that why you're mad?" Sassy handed Boon the last Chef Boyardee pizza.

"A man doesn't want his business advertised to every Tom, Dick, and Harry around here. People think things, and they don't ever get over it."

"I don't understand," Sassy said.

"How could you? Y'all got money."

"We ain't rich." Sassy picked up the grocery box. "You worried about what people think?"

Boon didn't answer.

"I won't say anything to anybody," Sassy said. "I'll make up some story. Daddy don't need to know."

Boon didn't speak for a minute, but his face relaxed a little. He smiled that heart-stopping smile. "You got a good heart, Sassy girl."

"Don't worry," Sassy said. "Daddy don't pay that much attention, anyway."

"I'll stop thinking about him this minute." Boon winked and punched her arm in a soft jab. "You know, you're okay for a kid."

A kid? Did Boon think she was a little girl? What about being her boyfriend?

"You could sing opera with that voice of yours," Boon said. "I heard it on the radio, and it kind of sounds like screaming."

But Sassy didn't even hear Boon's joke. Did he think she

was nothing but a little girl?

Just then, a pickup slowed and turned in the drive beside them. Sassy forgot Daddy drove home this way. He rolled down the window, looked at Boon with his arms full of groceries, and then spoke to Sassy. "Thought it was you," he said. "You okay?"

Sassy smiled big. "Right as rain," she said. "Got Boon here to walk from the Cheap Cash with me, but I spilled a Coke on my shirt." She slid the box sideways to show part of the stain.

Daddy looked at her for a long minute. "Why don't you jump on the back, and I'll take you on up to the house," he said. "Thanks, Boon. Appreciate the help." Daddy motioned to Sassy. She slipped the groceries into the bed of the truck, sat on the tailgate, and crossed her arms over her chest.

"See you later," she said to Boon.

The boy nodded as they turned down the dirt drive. Sassy watched him until Daddy parked the truck next to their back porch, but Boon never turned back to look. *Boon thought she was a little girl.*

Sassy jumped down and reached for the groceries, but Daddy came around and took them from her. "I thought you spilled your Coke," Daddy said, eyeing the empty paper cups stuck sideways among the groceries. "You buy another one?"

"Sort of. I bought two because I couldn't be rude and drink a Coke right in front of Boon, but I dropped them both in the mud before we got one sip," she said.

Daddy looked out to the road. "You don't need to prove anything when it comes to Boon," he said.

"I know." Sassy opened the screen door. "I was just being polite."

"Don't encourage that boy," Daddy said.

"I didn't," Sassy said. And she was happy when Daddy believed her.

6

Sassy's knife slipped off the slab of cold butter and made a loud, dull clang against the melamine plate. Daddy looked up but didn't speak, then went back to his pork chops and fried potatoes.

Sassy watched the vein in Daddy's temple pump in and out as he chewed; he hadn't said two words since they sat down. She was going to have to make up some kind of story to explain about the Cheap Cash. She sure didn't want Daddy to hear Mr. Frankie's side of the story.

"Pass the butter on around, please," Miss Dallas said. Sassy could feel the woman's gaze on her as she passed the butter dish, but Sassy didn't make eye contact. Miss Dallas was being nice as pie now. It was too late. How much trouble would it have been to answer a few simple questions about love? Stubborn old woman.

Sassy took a big bite of buttered bread and chewed with her mouth open. That would give Miss Dallas something to look at.

"Close your mouth," Miss Dallas said.

I'M NOT **EVER** FORGIVING HIM. NOT UNLESS HE ROMANCES ME WITH FLOWERS AND CANDLELIGHT AND SOFT MUSIC ON A MOON-DRENCHED TERRACE OVERLOOKING THE OCEAN. A LITTLE JEWELRY WOULDN'T HURT, EITHER.

"I wasn't smacking my food," Lula snapped back.

"I didn't say you were," Miss Dallas answered. "I was talking to Sassy."

Sassy held her hand to her cheek and yawned wide in a show just for Lula.

"That's disgusting!" Lula said. "Daddy, did you see her? Might as well have a pig at the supper table. "

"Hush," Miss Dallas said. "We don't need any name calling tonight."

Daddy sopped his biscuit around his plate as he spoke to Miss Dallas. "Can you come over early in the morning?" he asked.

"How early?"

"About six thirty. I need to go to a meeting at the tobacco auction." Daddy scooped up his potatoes with his gravy-soaked biscuit. "There was another editorial in this morning's *Courier Journal*. I wish to hell the government would stay out of our business. How do they expect us to make a living?"

The scrape of Miss Dallas's fork answered yes. She never told Daddy no.

Sassy listened to her back molars grind a tough bite of pork chop. Miss Dallas cooked worse than Granny on *The Beverly Hillbillies*. Sassy would have to tell her that sometime. She swigged a long drink of iced tea, then shoved her potatoes in her mouth and watched Daddy cut into his pork chop. She couldn't tell if Daddy was in a sorry mood or not.

To dodge Miss Dallas's questions, Sassy had changed her shirt the minute she walked into the house. She knew she needed to fess up about the charge ticket for Boon's groceries, but she wondered if she should try and talk to Daddy. How could Boon act so flirty, then call her a kid? Why would he do that?

Sassy stared at Daddy. He didn't look like the romantic type. His sandy brown hair swept into an ordinary pompadour, and his eyes were a regular shade of hazel, not unlike Sassy's. He sure wasn't tall, dark, and handsome. Mama said not one bit of a Romeo. At least, that was the story Miss Dallas always told.

Mama and Daddy met at Sunday brunch at the Brown Hotel in Louisville right before the end of the war. The whole hotel was swarming with people—not an empty table in the house—when Daddy and Uncle Dean asked Mama if they could sit down. Two soldier boys. Mama said no, but her girlfriend Louise made such a fuss, Mama changed her mind.

Two weeks later, Mama took the train to meet Daddy in San Antonio, Texas, and they were married the next day. It was real-life romance. Mama must have known she loved Daddy with all her heart. How else could she just up and leave home and take the train halfway across the country?

Daddy caught Sassy examining him, and she looked down at her plate. Daddy probably missed Mama too much to even think about romance. It was too sad. Sassy understood that.

After supper, Miss Dallas scraped the plates into the trash. "Lula, it's your turn for the dishes. There's a clean dishtowel in the drawer."

"It's not my turn! Sassy ran off in her bedroom last night and never did do her share. ..."

"Don't argue," Miss Dallas said. "She'll get to it, but tonight it's yours. Now, come on, do as I ask."

"Cinderella, do this! Cinderella, do that! Sassy never does a darn thing around here." Lula slammed the dishtowel drawer, but Miss Dallas just turned on the faucet and ignored her.

Sassy went outside and sat on the damp planks of the back porch. Daddy had already pulled their old agitator washing machine away from the wall and a leaking puddle of water. "Hand me that flathead screwdriver," he said.

Sassy flipped out the top tray of the toolbox and scoured

through the tools, looking for the screwdriver's yellow handle. "It's not here," she said.

"Well, I know it is. Shove that toolbox over here."

She pushed the metal box along the wood floor, and Daddy retrieved the screwdriver out of the top tray. "If it had been a snake, it would have bit you. Here, hold these."

Sassy cupped her hands to hold the loose screws from the washing machine's cover but dropped one and watched as it rolled under the hot-water heater.

"Sassy?"

"Sorry, Daddy. I'll get it." But she couldn't reach it. Before long, the broom handle was stuck under the hot-water heater, too, and Sassy had to ask Daddy to pull it out.

"Stop fooling around, Sassy, and pay attention if you're going to help me."

"Yes, sir."

"What's eating at you?"

"Nothing."

"Then watch what you're doing."

Sassy blew air out her lips in a long, slow sigh. "Daddy, I kind of need to tell you something," she said.

Daddy kept working. "What about?"

"I charged those two Cokes to your account at the Cheap Cash this afternoon. Mr. Frankie said you were good for it," she said. "I've got baby-sitting money to pay you back."

"Give it to Miss Dallas," Daddy said.

"And I bought me some other things, too."

"What do you mean?"

"Uh, female things ..." Sassy gave Daddy her best *you know* look. "Female things I needed! Miss Dallas didn't have them on her list, but I don't mind giving her the money." It was only a little white lie—female things didn't include Chef Boyardee pizza. But that way Daddy couldn't come back and say Sassy never told him she charged to the grocery ticket. Sassy could maneuver Miss Dallas later.

"You feeling okay?" Daddy asked.

"Fine," Sassy said. She smiled at Daddy.

"Female things …" Daddy repeated. "You're going to be a teenager before I know it."

Sassy wound her hair around her finger. "Is twelve a teenager?" Sassy asked. She would be twelve in a little more than a month.

"Not quite," Daddy said.

"You got to be thirteen?" Sassy asked. "But I feel like a teenager already."

"You do?"

"I mean, I don't feel like a little kid anymore, and I start junior high this fall."

"You got plenty of time," Daddy said. He wiped his hands on a handkerchief and pulled a circular carton of chewing tobacco from his hip pocket. He pressed a hefty pinch into his cheek.

"Were you still a teenager when you first met Mama?" Sassy knew the story already, but maybe Daddy wouldn't notice her questions about boys if she didn't ask him point-blank.

Daddy stopped for a moment and looked at her.

"When y'all first met?"

"That was a hundred years ago, Sassy."

"Just curious."

"I don't even remember," he said. He wiped his fingers on his knee and ran his tongue along the inside of his lip, then put the tobacco back into his pocket. "I guess I was nineteen—almost over being a teenager. Go on and get me that wrench on the floor," he said. Daddy worked to loosen the bolts of the motor's clutch.

Sassy waited for him to continue, but Daddy didn't say anything. She had to know how a boy fell in love with a girl. How else could she get Boon to fall for her? "So did you know right away she was the one?" she asked.

"Sassy, why are you asking all these questions?" Daddy said, snorting a little under his breath. "She was pretty. We were kids." He twirled the freed bolts with his fingers, and Sassy was careful to catch the wobbling metal. "There's nothing to tell."

"Did Mama ask you to be her boyfriend?"

"Not that I recall."

"Did you just worship the ground she walked on from the minute you set eyes on her?"

"Sassy, where do you get those ideas?"

Sassy jingled the bolts in her palm. "Did you ever tell Mama you wanted to just kiss her right on the lips?" Sassy laughed.

"Stop it, Sassy. I loved your mother. I told you that before." Daddy eased the clutch chain from around the drain pump.

"I forgot," Sassy lied.

"Why don't you go on in and see if Lula and Miss Dallas need any help." Daddy concentrated on his work.

"They say you know at first sight sometimes!" Sassy blurted out.

"Know what?" Daddy looked back at her.

"And you can't help yourself. It just happens. ..."

"What?"

"It's in all the magazines, Daddy."

"Sassy, what the heck are you talking about?"

"You know." Sassy didn't want to actually say the word *love*. It felt funny saying it out loud in front of Daddy somehow.

"Know what?" Daddy's voice was almost cross. He ran his hand along the chain, adjusting the drain pump as he went.

Sassy rolled the washing machine screws along the floor. "About feelings." She didn't dare look at Daddy. For a split second the evening air was still. Sassy could hear Lula talking too loud in the kitchen.

"You want to know about feelings?" Daddy sounded aggravated.

Sassy didn't say anything.

"You got *feelings* for some boy?" The sound of Daddy's voice echoed into the yard.

"No!"

"Boon Chisholm?"

"No!" Sassy stared right back at Daddy. "I'm never acting nice again. All I get is griped out about it!" She twisted her hair until a tangle caught her finger. "But *Love Confessions* says that …"

Daddy didn't let her finish. "Scat, girl! I'm taking every one of those romance magazines in your room and throwing them right in the trash! We ain't having this conversation."

Sassy spoke louder than she meant to. "I just want to know about boys! I don't have a mama to talk to! How else am I going to find out things if nobody tells me?"

"What makes you think you're old enough to go off with some boy? You're eleven years old! A boy won't do anything but get you in trouble, and I don't want any grandbabies around here."

"I don't want to know about *that*!" Sassy said. She'd die before she'd ask Daddy anything about *that*. "I just want to know how you and Mama fell in love."

"So you're in *love* now?" Daddy's face screwed up sarcastic and bitter.

"No!"

"So what do you want to know?"

"You said you adored Mama. I just want to know about how a boy falls in love with a girl. How did you know for a positive fact you loved Mama? How did you know?"

"That's for you to find out in about ten years, young lady.

You've got no business knowing now." Daddy spit the juice of his chewing tobacco into an empty Coca-Cola bottle. "Go in the house and help Miss Dallas. Stop thinking about this."

Tears started up behind Sassy's eyes.

"Hand me those bolts before you go in," Daddy said.

Sassy gathered up the loose bolts. "Here." Sassy bit the inside of her cheek to keep from crying.

Daddy spoke quiet, without looking at her. "I'm not raising a runaround little tart. Those magazines give you bad ideas. I want them in the burn barrel by morning."

Sassy pushed open the back door. Daddy talked like love was something wicked. How in the world did he romance Mama into marrying him?

Sassy skirted around the kitchen into the hallway without Miss Dallas seeing her. She threw herself onto her bed, pulled out her magazine, and opened to the page she had dog-eared last night: "The Love Test: How Well Do You Really Know Him?" She didn't know Boon's favorite color, his most cherished possession, or his deepest secret. And she didn't know how to find out without asking him—she couldn't do that. Sassy slid the magazine under the sheet. Who in the world could she ask about love?

Sassy hated it like the devil, but there was only one person in the house who had boyfriend experience. She had to talk to Lula.

7

The next morning, Miss Dallas pointed out the goose grass in the vegetable garden. Sassy and Lula had orders to do the weeding while Miss Dallas took food to an elderly widow in town, but the minute she left, Lula hauled out a quilt and sat cross-legged in the grass with her nose stuck in some book.

Sassy threw a handful of cockleburs in Lula's direction. "What are you reading?" she asked.

"Nothing you would like." Lula never looked up.

"You're supposed to be helping me."

"I dried the dinner dishes last night." Lula turned the page.

Sassy gathered a stockpile of weeds into a worn-out plastic bucket and glanced over at her sister. How could she get Lula talking about boyfriends? "You read that stupid book last summer—you still reading on it?"

Lula closed her book and sighed long and slow. "I'm *re*reading it," she said as she parted her ponytail and pulled it tight against her

So WE GOT IN A

FIGHT,

AND SHE

PULLED OUT HALF

MY HAIR.

I POPPED HER

GOOD, RIGHT

IN THE MOUTH.

SHE WON'T BE

MESSING WITH MY

BOYFRIEND AGAIN.

head. "I finished it last summer, but I wanted to read it again—you wouldn't know about that since you never read."

"I read magazines!" Sassy stuck her weeding knife into the dirt and a dandelion root popped up.

"I rest my case. Your stupid romance magazines don't count."

"And your stupid romance novels do?"

Lula laid the book next to her and spun her ponytail into a bun on the back of her head.

Sassy ripped another dandelion out of the dirt, then wiped her weeding knife on her shorts. "So, what's that book about?"

"A poor, plain girl named Jane Eyre who takes a job baby-sitting a rich man's daughter, then secretly falls in love with him."

"She nicer than Miss Dallas?" Sassy bent over to pick up the book, but Lula jerked it away.

"You're hands are dirty," she said. She slid it over to the far corner of the quilt, then stood up. "Jane's not nearly as nosy; that's why she doesn't find out about his wife." Lula dragged the rake through the sweet peppers.

"He's married?" Sassy asked. "Does his wife get mad?"

"Jane thinks she's dead."

"Like Mama?"

Lula stopped. "Why do you have to bring Mama up all the time? You don't even remember her. Mama's dead—she's not coming back."

"You don't have to talk so mean about Mama," Sassy said.

Lula shut up and attacked the sweet peppers with the rake. Sassy turned on the hose and rinsed her hands under the water. "What does Jane do? If she loves him …" She waved her hands in the air to dry them.

"She about marries him, but she finds out the truth. His wife is crazy."

"Why would he try to trick Jane like that?"

"Because he loves her."

"But he's married." Sassy picked up the book and thumbed through the last few pages.

"You're such a baby, Sassy; he loves Jane, and he's married to this loony woman. He's miserable with his wife."

"It's like in *Love Confessions*, then," Sassy said. "People get confused about love, but then they come to their senses. Love conquers all."

"It's not like that one bit," Lula said. "It's a real love story." She leaned on the rake.

Sassy tossed the book on the blanket. "*Love Confessions* stories are real love stories. They don't make them up."

Lula gave Sassy a look of sheer disgust. "They do, too."

"How do you know?"

"Because I just know," Lula said. She let the rake flop beside a muskmelon and sat down on the quilt next to Sassy.

"How?"

"Are you some broken record? I've read your stupid magazines, and love is nothing like that."

This was Sassy's chance to get Lula talking. "Well, what's it like?"

Lula picked a bouquet of yellow dandelions and hesitated as if she didn't know if she should answer. "Heaven. Better than heaven."

Sassy leaned toward her sister. "Are you in love?" she asked.

"I never said that. …" Lula was cross again.

"What about Elgin McNatt?"

"What are you talking about?" Lula demanded.

"Did you love him?"

Elgin, football captain and man-about-town, had actually kissed Lula right on the lips last year—in front of her locker and a whole hall full of kids. Lula was worse than a bad actress and told Daddy that she never provoked that kiss. Sassy knew Lula lied.

"Him? I never even liked Elgin."

"You never felt nothing for him?" Sassy asked. "Not even when he kissed you? Didn't your insides get all nervous?"

A smug little smile crossed Lula's lips. "Do you have a crush on somebody?" she asked.

"No."

Lula sang under her breath. "Sassy's got a boyfriend!"

"I do not!" Sassy grabbed Lula's arm in an Indian burn.

"Stop that! It hurts!"

Sassy let go. She wasn't getting anywhere with Lula. She went back to weeding.

"I can't help it that I've got lots of boyfriends," Lula said. "Maybe it's because I don't go beating them up."

"None of your stupid boyfriends are worth having," Sassy said. She stabbed at the blades of goose grass.

"That you know about," Lula said.

Sassy looked over at her sister. "I'm going to tell Daddy."

"Go right ahead. I bet Daddy would love to know that you kissed Reeves Hanvey. If you go tattling, no telling what Daddy might find out."

Sassy clinched the weeding knife in her hand. "You better not go squealing."

"I'm not saying a thing," Lula said. She lay back on the quilt. "I don't want him yelling any more than you do."

Sassy sat down next to Lula. Maybe this was her chance. "How do you know if a boy likes you? I mean, really likes you?" Her voice was no more than a whisper.

A hint of surprise softened Lula's face. For a split second, she seemed like a real sister.

"I'll dry the dinner dishes every night for a month," Sassy offered.

"I'm not sure I know," Lula said. She frowned, but that didn't

keep her from being pretty. "Sometimes, I think boys like you more if they're not sure how you feel about them. It's kind of weird." Lula seemed lost in her thoughts for a moment. "It helps if you're cute, I guess."

"What does that mean?"

Lula sat up. "Boys like *girls*. Maybe you could start pretending to be one. Wear a dress once in a while. Clean up some. Take a bath."

Lula's words stung Sassy deep. "You think I stink?" Sassy yelled. "I don't need any beauty advice from you. Who says a boy wants a prissy girl?"

A knowing look crossed Lula's face. "You *do* have a boyfriend!"

"No I don't!"

Lula's voice turned singsongy. "Sassy's got a boyfriend! Sassy's got a boyfriend!"

"I said to stop, and I mean it!"

Lula smiled real sweet. "Sassy's got a boyfriend!"

In one quick move, Sassy threw down her weeding knife and wrestled Lula facedown onto the quilt, pinning her sister's arms beneath her. She pressed one knee into Lula's shoulder blade.

"Let me up!" Lula squirmed worse than a grass snake. "What do you want?"

"Tell me about your boyfriends. Tell me about Elgin."

"I never even liked Elgin McNatt!" Lula kicked her feet and tried to squeeze out of Sassy's hold.

"Lula, you better start telling the truth!" Sassy pushed her knee forward.

"Sassy's got a boyfriend!"

Sassy grabbed up the sharp side of the weeding knife and held it close to Lula's ponytail. "You sing that again, and I'll chop your hair off."

Lula shrieked, but Sassy pressed harder. The weeding knife

caught in the tangled strands of Lula's prized ponytail. A soft gnawing sound, like the cutting of a supple rope, hinted at what was happening.

"Get off me!" Lula bent her knees and kicked her feet up behind her, right into the small of Sassy's back. She struggled to free her hands, but Sassy held tight.

"Tell me everything you know about getting boys to like you. Start with Elgin," Sassy said.

The gnawing became louder, and Lula kicked Sassy again.

"Start talking! Tell me!"

Lula blubbered out a scream. "I liked him, and I wanted him to kiss me."

"Did you tell him that?"

"No! He just knew. From the way I acted." Lula looked back at Sassy. There was a worried look in her eye.

"How did you know he liked you?" Sassy leaned back on her sister's torso and threw the weeding knife far out into the grass so Lula couldn't find it. Lula relaxed her head a little.

"Same thing. He teased me about reading books and walked me home from school almost every day for a month."

Boon had teased Sassy.

"Finally, I just asked him," Lula said.

"You asked him right out?"

"I did, and he admitted it. Said he liked me," Lula said. "He must have told the truth, because he kissed me the next day." Lula twisted underneath Sassy and tried to push her away. "You got a crush on somebody, don't you? Tell me. I won't tell Daddy, I promise."

"Your nose is growing longer than Pinocchio's, Lula. You're going to ruin that pretty face." A breeze stirred up and wisps of Lula's hair flew across the garden. "If I let you up, will you behave?" Sassy asked.

Lula nodded.

"You better behave, now." Sassy pulled herself up quick.

Lula sat up and reached for her ponytail. Some of it was still there. She pulled the rubber band from the back of her head, and a tangled bunch of hair and grass came out in her hand. Lula jumped up. Only about half of her hair was long; the rest barely reached her left shoulder. "Look what you did! You cut my hair!"

"Well, you started it," Sassy said. "It wasn't my fault."

"My hair! You cut off my hair!" Lula pulled what was left of her long hair around her shoulder. "It's gone. It's all gone." Her voice made a raspy, grating sound that edged on tears.

"That's what you get for being so selfish," Sassy said.

"You brat!" It was as if Lula finally understood what Sassy had done. Lula held the gold clump of ponytail in her outstretched hands. "You mean little brat!" In an instant, Lula's face transformed from disbelief to wild anger. She threw down the ball of grass and hair. "You just wait. I'm going to watch you until I find out who your little boyfriend is, and I'm going to tell Daddy all about how you're running around behind his back."

"You should have stopped singing about me having a boyfriend when I told you to!" Sassy yelled. "You'd still have a ponytail."

"You're going to regret this!"

Sassy tried to grab Lula's arm, but Lula jerked away and ran up the path to the tobacco barn. "You're the one who thinks love's *like heaven!*" Sassy called after her. "You're the one with the boyfriend!"

But Lula didn't answer. Her lopsided hair shined in the morning sun.

8

DARLING,
DARLING,
I ADORE YOU. I'LL
LOVE YOU FOR
THE REST
OF MY LIFE.
I MUST HAVE
WRITTEN IT
IN JUST THOSE
WORDS—WITH A
LILTING, LOOPY
HANDWRITING,
SEALED WITH
A KISS.

Sassy watched to see if Lula would come sneaking back into the yard, but she didn't. Finally, Sassy tramped around and found the weeding knife and hung it on the hook in the shed. She rifled through the kitchen drawer to find the stub of a pencil and a yellowed school tablet.

She wasn't about to wait around for Lula's return. Sassy ran across the road and ended up under an ancient pin oak a quarter mile away from the house, not far from the bowstring bridge that crossed the deepest part of the Rough River. Daddy said that tree had been there since George Washington owned this part of Kentucky.

Sassy sat on an arched-out tree root with the tablet and pencil in her lap. So what if she had stole the whole idea from Lula—it was a good one. She would tell Boon she liked him—not in person, of course. In a love letter. That would get the ball rolling. Then, Boon could tell her he never really thought she was a little girl, and that he secretly had a crush on her all along,

even if she was ever so slightly younger than he was. Maybe he would even kiss her.

Sassy would have the cutest boyfriend in Grayson County, and Lula would end up with a bunch of no-count Reeves Hanvey boyfriends. Poor lovelorn Lula. Sassy could hardly hold back a big cry for her sister.

Sassy stared at the blank page. What should she tell Boon? She couldn't just write *I love you, Boon Hoyt Chisholm*. Not on a plain old tablet, and she didn't have any nice paper. It was so easy in *Love Confessions*, but now Sassy couldn't think.

Finally, she wrote in her best cursive handwriting:

My dearest Boon,

My dearest. Would Boon laugh? Sassy erased it. *Dearest* sounded like something Lula would say—or maybe that silly Jane Eyre. Sassy tried again in a large loopy script.

Boon, darling ...

Darlings—dearly loved persons. People called each other *darling* all the time in the movies, but it looked cartoony when she saw it written on the paper. Maybe it was easier to call a person *darling* when you were speaking to them. Or in a movie with them. Sassy erased, but the pencil mark smudged, and a tiny hole ate its way into the page. She tore the paper off the tablet and crushed it into a ball.

Boon: Roses are red and violets are blue.
Can you guess who likes you?

But what if Boon couldn't guess? What if a lot of girls liked

him? Sassy couldn't think of that now. The paper fluttered in a gust of hot August breeze.

Finally, she drew a heart on clean paper and wrote in a clear, solid hand.

Sassy folded the page into a tiny square and tucked it in the pocket of her dungarees. She could give the paper to Boon and just let him read it. She didn't have to say a word. Sassy hid the tablet, the wad of paper, and the pencil behind a large tree root and headed out for the mile walk to Boon's front porch.

It didn't take fifteen minutes to get to Boon's house. Sassy had never set foot on the Chisholm place, and she imagined Miss Dallas would have a cat if she knew Sassy were there now. Sassy would forget to tell her.

Every door and window in the house was wide open, but in the heat of the day there wasn't a breeze anywhere. Sassy knocked and peered in through the screen. The morning's cereal bowls were still on the coffee table, and an old cotton bedspread hung over the divan. The house was quiet, but she could hear kids hollering around back. Sassy listened and knocked louder, but the sound echoed through the small, ramshackle house. There was no one inside. A little girl's laughter drifted along from the backyard, then a baby cried. Somebody was home.

Around back, Boon's twin brothers had an old bicycle down in the field below the house. The boys took turns playing barechested broncobuster, making the bicycle pitch and wheelie its

way around the field, entertaining Boon's little sisters, who sat on the porch bouncing the baby between their laps. Not one of them had on shoes, and Sassy could smell the acid odor of the baby's diaper all the way over to where she stood.

Mrs. Chisholm stood by a low chicken-wire fence surrounded by a puny plot of field peas and sweet potatoes. She didn't see Sassy, and in another minute Sassy would have been halfway back to the road, but Mrs. Chisholm cocked her head and looked up just as Sassy started to turn and run.

"Hello!" she called out.

Sassy was caught.

"Hello?"

"Hey, Mrs. Tipps," Sassy spoke a little too loud.

"There ain't no Mrs. Tipps here anymore," she said. The lines around her mouth deepened. "She's free of that lying son-of-a-gun."

Sassy didn't answer. "Is Boon home?"

Mrs. Chisholm smiled Boon's smile, but her teeth were yellowed.

"I'm Sassy Thompkins."

"I know who you are."

Sassy had heard Miss Dallas say that Boon's mama's looks had been lost on babying and bourbon. Mrs. Chisholm's black hair was teased into a round bouffant, and Sassy could see Boon in her, but it was a faded, worn version. "He's over to Caneyville. Be back shortly," Mrs. Chisholm said.

"Nice garden you got there."

"No need to lie about it; I ain't that gullible. The plants is puny, but I never did exactly take to field work." Mrs. Chisholm took a cigarette and lighter out of her pocket. She flicked on the lighter a time or two until the flame caught.

"Daddy's got some work in the barn if Boon wants it." Sassy's

lie rolled out of her mouth like it was the truth.

"Do you want to wait a few minutes?" Mrs. Chisholm said, blowing a long coil of cigarette smoke into the air. "Boon'll be back directly, I imagine."

"Well, maybe," Sassy said. "But I can't wait long."

"How's your daddy?" Both twins were on the bike now, howling as the front wheel upended and sent them tumbling. The girls ran out to meet them, the baby bouncing on the older girl's hip.

"Good," Sassy said. "Busy."

"Miss Dallas?"

"Good, too," Sassy said.

Mrs. Chisholm inhaled a long drag off her cigarette.

"Sure is hot," Sassy said. She worried over the note in her pocket. Why in tarnation did Mrs. Chisholm want to stand here and chitchat? Didn't she have something else to do?

"It is that." Mrs. Chisholm rubbed out the stub of her cigarette into the dirt, then put it in her pocket. "Might need some smokes later," she said. "You say your daddy's doing good?" A halfhearted smile softened her face. "He seems like a nice man, your daddy."

"Thank you. I'll tell him you said hello." Another lie.

"You do that. Maybe we could all get together for a picnic sometime? You kids, and your daddy, and me. I always thought it was such a waste your mama died. Seems like she was just here one day and gone the next. Cancer, wasn't it?"

Sassy nodded.

"Must be lonely for your daddy. I can understand that."

Something about the velvet sound of Mrs. Chisholm's voice made Sassy's stomach gurgle up funny.

An argument brewed over the bicycle. The smallest of the girls wailed and made her way up the path.

"You like little kids, Sassy?" Mrs. Chisholm asked.

"Not all that much," Sassy said.

Mrs. Chisholm laughed. "Ever baby-sit?"

"Sometimes."

"Well, I might just hire you if you're willing to work cheap. Go get myself a little fun." Mrs. Chisholm raised her eyebrows. "But don't you go spreading that around." Sassy didn't hear any joy in her voice.

By that time, the other kids were stomping up the path, too, the bicycle abandoned. The little girl was still bawling her lungs out, and snot poured out her nose. Mrs. Chisholm picked up the girl and wiped her nose with the palm of her own hand while the little girl hollered.

"Lord of mercy, I wish I never had kids," Mrs. Chisholm said.

Sassy bit her lip. She could bet that most days the kids probably weren't too wild about the arrangement, either. "I'll guess I'll try to catch up with Boon later," Sassy said.

At that moment the Chisholm's old rusted Ford pickup turned into the backyard and sputtered to a stop. "I knew he wouldn't be long," Mrs. Chisholm said. "Boon, baby," she called. "You got you some company here, darling."

9

ALWAYS PLAY HARD TO GET. **KEEP HIM GUESSING,** AND NEVER TELL HIM WHAT YOU'RE REALLY FEELING. THAT'S HOW TO SNAG A MAN.

Boon slammed the door of the truck. "Where's the party?" he asked. "Morning, Sassy. I haven't seen you in ages, girl." Boon grinned.

Sassy stared at Boon longer than she meant to. Maybe Mrs. Chisholm didn't notice. "Daddy has some work up to the barn and said you could come over and help if you wanted. Told me to come tell you." Sassy hated to get Boon's hopes up about work, but how else could she have an excuse to talk to him?

Mrs. Chisholm listened.

"Said to say he'll pay good." She had to give the letter to Boon. It had to be now.

Mrs. Chisholm spoke to Boon. "Did you bring something for these kids to eat?"

"All they handed out was rat cheese." Boon handed her a worn brown sack from the back of the pickup. One of the twins grabbed at the bag, but Mrs. Chisholm yanked his arm up and shoved the boy into the house.

"Get in there!" she shouted.

"Thanks for letting me wait," Sassy said.

"Anytime," Mrs. Chisholm said. "Be sure and tell your daddy hello."

Mrs. Chisholm scooted the kids into the house, and Sassy could hear plates clanging from the kitchen, then more crying.

Boon tipped his hat back on his head. "We meet again," he said.

A shyness caught hold of Sassy, and she didn't know what to say. She smiled. Boon smiled.

"Want some chewing gum?" Boon fished a yellow strip from his pocket. He smelled like sweet tobacco.

"No, thanks," Sassy said. "Miss Dallas doesn't like me and Lula chewing gum, and I'm headed home."

"Don't want to get on Miss Dallas's bad side." Boon chuckled and slid the gum back into his pocket. "That woman will put the evil eye on you for sure." Boon turned on the water faucet at the end of the house, rubbed his hands against the clean current of water, and splashed his face. He wiped the water away from his eyes.

Sassy glanced into the house and talked in a low voice. "I lied. Daddy didn't send me," she said. "He don't have any work. I'm sorry." She handed the note to Boon. "But here."

Boon sat down on the steps and dried his hands on his pants. He started to unfold the paper. "Is this from …?"

"From me! But don't open it!" Sassy whispered. She peeked over her shoulder and caught Mrs. Chisholm looking out the window. "Don't be looking at it now. It's personal."

"Well, girl, if I'm the person it's personal for, why can't I open it?"

"You just can't. Not till I leave."

Boon glanced over his shoulder and spoke in a loud voice. "When do I need to be over at y'all's place?"

"Oh, uh, this afternoon, I guess," Sassy said, matching his volume.

"Sassy Thompkins, what are you up to?" Boon's eyes narrowed. "Tell me what you come to say."

Sassy grabbed the paper back from him. "It says I like you. That's all. I mean, it doesn't *say* that. There's a heart with my initials and your initials and a plus sign, but that's what it means. That I like you, Boon. I like you real good." Sassy waited. "Do you like me back?" She waited again for his reply.

Just then, the twins came roaring out the back door, and Mrs. Chisholm called from the kitchen. "Hurry up out there!"

Boon stomped the mud off his boots. His voice was loud again for Mrs. Chisholm's benefit. "Sure thing, I'll come by in the morning."

The twins hung on to Boon's legs. "Guess we better go in." He smiled that heartbreaking smile. "Thanks for stopping by, Sassy. Tell your daddy I appreciate him thinking of me."

Didn't Boon hear what she said? Sassy shoved the paper back in her pocket, and sour bile came up from her stomach. Boon didn't like her? He ignored her question!

Sassy ran. She ran halfway down the dirt drive to the road, scolding herself for spilling her heart to Boon. This was Lula's stupid idea. Why did she even listen to her in the first place?

"Sassy!"

Lula probably lied. She probably never asked Elgin a thing.

"Sassy!"

Boon flirted with lots of girls. He didn't think anything about her—except that Sassy was a silly little girl with a crush. Her throat felt tight, and her eyes hurt. Why had she been in such a hurry to tell him she liked him? This was all Lula's fault.

"Sassy! Wait up!"

Sassy stopped dead in her tracks. Boon came up behind her.

"Take this piece of Juicy Fruit," he said. He pressed the gum into her hand. "You can have it later. Just don't tell Miss Dallas."

"I don't want your silly Juicy Fruit. Didn't you hear what I said?" She couldn't breathe. "Why didn't you say something?"

Boon bent down to catch her gaze. His eyes were the color of sweet violets she had once ironed between pieces of waxed paper.

"You are one curious girl, Sassy Thompkins." He shook his head, and this time his smile seemed to apologize a little for her hurt. "Don't be asking a man to tell you how he feels. You might take him by surprise and get him all nervous."

"But you don't like me anyhow, so what does it matter? You think I'm just a stupid little kid."

"Did I ever say that?"

"Not exactly. You told me yesterday, 'You're okay for a kid,' but it's the same thing."

"It is?"

"What am I supposed to think?"

Boon sighed and shook his head. "Sassy, Sassy, Sassy. You have a mighty unusual way of thinking on things. You might need to quit worrying so much."

"So now I'm pushy?"

"I didn't say that."

"I'm pushy and stupid and sour-faced? Is that why you don't want to be my boyfriend?" Sassy's voice broke. She didn't want to cry in front of Boon.

"What? What are you talking about? Lord, girl, you just don't pay one bit of mind, do you?" Boon didn't hide his grin. "I'm already—"

"Stop smiling."

"I'm trying to tell you—"

"Stop talking. But why did you flirt with me and let me buy

your groceries if you didn't like me? You just led me on."

"That's not fair. You're the one who butted in and made it your business."

"But I thought ..."

"Sassy, you hunting for a boyfriend?"

"No! I mean, I thought ..."

"I don't know what to say exactly ..."

Sassy felt the tears coming up around her eyes. So Boon thought she was chasing him like some desperate lovesick fool? She wouldn't give him the satisfaction of crying right there. She ran as hard as she could.

"Don't run away!" Boon yelled behind her. "Sassy! Sassy!" But Boon's voice was distant now.

She ran to the pin oak and never looked back. Boys! She hated them all. Breathless, Sassy threw the Juicy Fruit at the tree and collapsed into the grass.

Boon didn't come looking for her. He must be about the meanest boy in all of Kentucky. Maybe even the world. Sassy took the note out of her pocket and unfolded the paper. She found a stick and stabbed it into the note until a dozen holes poked into the dirt and the paper was nothing but a shred of yellow tablet, unrecognizable.

Sassy's humiliation caught up in her chest, making a salty taste in her throat. If only Mama were alive. Her mama would love her, even if she wasn't pretty enough for some stupid boyfriend. Mama would never be like that worthless Mrs. Chisholm who hated her own children.

Sassy wiped her eyes in the bend of her arm and lay back into the grass. Sometimes in *Love Confessions*, the plain girls got the boys to fall in love with them, but then they usually were just pretty girls in disguise. Boon would never love her. She wasn't good-looking enough. Mama and Daddy had passed all the pretty parts on to Lula before Sassy was even born. Maybe they never planned on having another daughter.

Sassy lay still in the grass until all the tears were gone, and a numb hurt settled over her. Is this how a heartache felt? A thin pain shot through her back with every breath. She imagined her heart in pieces in her chest.

Finally, Sassy sat up and blew her nose into the hem of her shirt and gathered up the tablet and the balled-up paper and the pencil from the base of the pin oak. She almost stepped on the chewing gum but picked it up and shoved it into her pocket.

Lula had probably showed off her missing ponytail by now, and Miss Dallas would have a switch all trimmed and ready for Sassy's legs. She started home.

Lula would always be the beautiful sister with all the boy-friends. That was just the God's honest truth, and there was no getting even with God. No switch could hurt more than that.

10

A GOOD GIRL
NEVER CALLS
A BOY ON THE
TELEPHONE OR
GOES OVER TO
HIS HOUSE.
SHE DOESN'T
DATE UNTIL SHE
TURNS SIXTEEN
AND DOESN'T GO
STEADY WITHOUT
HER PARENTS'
PERMISSION.
SHE'S NOT FLIRTY.
AND SHE'S NEVER
FORWARD.

Miss Dallas met Sassy at the gate. Instead of a switch, she carried a thonged rubber sandal in her hand. Sassy managed to skip aside most of the sandal's stinging whelps, until Miss Dallas shooed her up the porch steps into the kitchen, and Lula jumped into the fray with a pair of pinking shears.

Even though Miss Dallas turned the sandal on Lula, too, when it was all said and done, zig-zagged hanks of Sassy's hair ended up scattered all over the linoleum, along with a strap ripped from the sandal's sole.

Miss Dallas finally wrestled the scissors from Lula and ordered Sassy into her bedroom for starting the whole haircut feud in the first place. No matter it was Lula's fault entirely. Lula was sentenced to do the supper dishes, and both girls would get their just punishment as soon as Daddy got home.

Although the windows were up, Sassy's room was warm. An ancient box fan struggled to move the air, while the late afternoon sun slid down the wall and along the bedspread. Sassy flipped through the last pages of *Love Confessions*, ignoring the love test altogether.

Miss Dallas yelled from the kitchen. "Sassy!"

Sassy didn't answer. She didn't want to end up like Miss Dallas, fighting other people's kids for money and something to do. But what kind of romance could you hope for if you were a plain girl? A man with a crazy wife, like that desperate Jane Eyre?

"Sassy!" Miss Dallas knocked on her bedroom door but didn't wait for a reply before walking in. She tossed a paper bag onto the bed. "You need to get those romance magazines out to the burn barrel before your daddy gets home."

Sassy slipped the *Love Confessions* back under her pillow.

"Hurry up now," Miss Dallas said.

Sassy swung her legs over the edge of the bed, and Miss Dallas handed her a stack of magazines from the chair.

"Don't fiddle around."

Working in slow motion, Sassy piled all the magazines from the chair into the brown bag. When the bag was finally full and in the middle of Sassy's bedroom floor, Miss Dallas reached over and pulled the last magazine out from under Sassy's pillow and pitched it on top of the stack.

Sassy started to argue, but a certain look from Miss Dallas told her to forget it.

"You think with all that trash reading you do, you wouldn't be asking questions about love all the time," Miss Dallas said.

"What would you know about it?" Sassy bounced back onto the bed. "You never even read one story from any of those magazines. Never even been in love. You said so yourself."

"Said I didn't want to put up with a man," Miss Dallas corrected. "They're too much trouble. But I never said a thing about my love life."

"So you actually been in love?"

"That seem impossible to you?"

Sassy eyed Miss Dallas with a serious look of doubt. The woman ignored her.

"So Lula tells me you got some boyfriend," Miss Dallas said. "Not that I care about your business."

Miss Dallas would be clam-happy to know all of Sassy's personal business.

"Well, just for the record, I don't have no boyfriend," Sassy said. "I don't even know how you get a boyfriend. And I don't want to know." But something cracked in her voice.

"Then, why are you asking me and your daddy and Lula and God knows who every question you can think of about romance?" Miss Dallas sat down on the bed next to Sassy. "Sit up, and let me look at the damage."

Sassy felt the woman part the back of her hair. "Lula did a good job," Miss Dallas said. "You've about got a bald spot right in the center, but it's underneath. You could wear your hair in one big braid." Miss Dallas raked her fingers through Sassy's hair and started to braid the strands. "Probably never even see the spot then."

For a minute, Sassy liked the feel of hands working the braid of her hair. Miss Dallas was being nice—understanding, even. But Sassy still had a few lingering red marks on the back of her legs. Miss Dallas could try all she wanted, but she still wasn't a mama. Mamas didn't go after kids with sandals.

"You're growing up, Sassy," Miss Dallas said. "One day you'll have a boyfriend and start going out on dates and the whole shebang. But you got to start behaving like a young lady. A boy don't want some wild girl that might get after him with a weeding knife."

Sassy didn't say anything.

"I don't have a ribbon, but hold on to the braid and go over there and take a look." Miss Dallas pushed the bag of magazines along the floor to the foot of Sassy's bed. "You'd almost look pretty with your hair like that," she said. "If you would get that hair washed …"

Sassy looked in the mirror.

Miss Dallas got up to leave but stood behind Sassy and held the girl's braid. Their reflected eyes exchanged glances in the mirror.

"So you been in love before?" Sassy asked.

"One time," Miss Dallas said. Something soft crossed Miss Dallas's face until Sassy almost felt bad for bringing it up.

"Okay," Miss Dallas said. "Two questions about romance. That's all."

Sassy took a deep breath.

"Oh, and don't for one minute expect this to be a free lunch," Miss Dallas said. "You got to do something in return."

"What?" Sassy untangled the braid and ran her hands through her hair, then tucked it behind her ears.

"You got to start acting like a young woman. Not some hillbilly holy terror."

Sassy wiped her nose on the back of her hand. "What does that mean?"

"No loud ugly talk and no fighting."

Sassy nodded.

"No back sassing. No running off whenever you please. And no big, fat lying to my face like it was the truth."

Sassy considered it. "Does Lula have to act nice, too?"

"That does not concern you, little missy." Miss Dallas waited.

Sassy let out a long sigh, picked up her brush, and sat down on the chair once reserved for the *Love Confessions* magazines.

"What makes a boy like a girl?"

Miss Dallas didn't hesitate. "A lot of things. Sometimes it's looks. Sometimes personality. Sometimes there's no good reason. It just happens. Chemistry, they call it."

"Chemistry?"

"Sometimes a girl gives out a signal," Miss Dallas said. "A certain look. A twinkle in her eye. A smile. And a boy likes what he sees."

"Because she's pretty?" Sassy asked.

"Is that your second question?" Miss Dallas looked at her watch.

"No! You can't count that!"

"Not always. Ever heard that beauty is in the eye of the beholder? Boys like different things in girls. But a girl can't command a boy to like her. It don't work that way," Miss Dallas said. "You can't be self-centered and forward. Boys don't like forward girls blurting out their feelings and demanding attention. Boys like nice young ladies with polite manners. Remember that."

Sassy nodded.

"Now, what else?" Miss Dallas waited.

"Give me a minute! I got to pick out the best one to ask!" Sassy pulled the brush through her hair. "Let me think."

"Well, hurry, because I'm in the middle of making supper."

"How do you know it's real love?" Sassy asked. "How did my mama know she loved Daddy enough to just up and leave home and get married?"

Miss Dallas leaned on the dresser. "My guess is she didn't know. You don't know for years if it's real love. And then one day, it just is or it isn't."

"But how did she know in the beginning? A girl's got to know from the start if it's real." Sassy searched Miss Dallas's face for some hint, some clue, something.

"Hwhoo! Who told you that?" Miss Dallas asked. "You read it in one of those magazines?"

Sassy sighed. "Were you in real love?"

Miss Dallas frowned. "That's your third question, so you're done."

"Wait!" Sassy had more than two questions. She had more than two hundred questions. "You didn't answer all that good! You didn't tell me one single detail."

Miss Dallas didn't wait. She turned down the hall to the kitchen. "Get those magazines outside, right now. Then set the table." The woman disappeared.

Sassy sighed. "Thanks for nothing!" she yelled. Then, she locked her door and rifled through the *Love Confessions* to find her two favorite copies, along with the love test issue. She stuffed them in her underwear drawer and bounced back on the bed.

Is that what Boon meant? He wanted a nice girl that wasn't pushy? Sassy thought about it. He *did* come after her when she had run away. He *did* say she was almost pretty when she wasn't so sour-faced. He *did* say he might kiss her.

She searched for the Juicy Fruit in her pocket. She fingered the wrapper and then breathed deep. It had a faint aroma of mint and sugar. Was the Juicy Fruit her first official boyfriend present?

Miss Dallas hollered from the kitchen.

Sassy sat up and pulled her hair back. She'd never have the patience for some fancy do-up braid. She rooted around in her drawer and found a pair of old school scissors and lopped off the long ends of her hair until it curved around her face.

Sassy stood up before the mirror and ruffled her fingers through her hair. It was still her, but an almost grown-up girl looked back at her. Sassy hid her face in her hands but stole another look in the mirror. She smiled. Was she pretty? Was she beautiful?

11

> **I** DOLLED UP WITH EYELINER AND LIPSTICK, AND TEASED MY HAIR INTO THE PERFECT FLIP. THE MIRROR SAID I WAS THE **PRETTIEST** GIRL IN TOWN. BUT DID HE NOTICE?

Sassy yanked the last wild onion out of the vegetable garden, raked the weeds into a pile, then hauled the whole mess to the burn barrel. Scattered *Love Confessions* were strewn through the scorched trash and last night's supper scraps.

After hearing Miss Dallas's prattle on about the haircut fight, Daddy had condemned Sassy to weed the entire vegetable garden alone, while Lula ironed every last shirt in the clothes basket.

As soon as the breakfast dishes were done, Sassy got to work on the garden's stubborn goose grass, and now she was finished. The morning sun was almost straight up in the sky, and she was wet with sweat. Sassy opened the back porch screen and held the door until it closed behind her.

"Thank you," Miss Dallas said. "I love not hearing that screen door slam." She spoke in a matter-of-fact voice from the kitchen table where she was pasting Green Stamps into a redemption booklet.

Sassy put her lips directly to the kitchen faucet and sucked the cold water into her mouth until she caught Miss Dallas's scowl. She wiped her mouth on a kitchen towel. "Where's Lula?"

"In her room," Miss Dallas said. "We had to even up her pony-tail a good bit. Says she's sick, but she's going to get well here in a few minutes. She's still got those shirts to iron." Miss Dallas looked up over her glasses. "Your haircut turned out real cute. You like it?"

"Maybe."

Miss Dallas had trimmed up Sassy's handiwork. Now the girl's hair was bobbed close to her head in shaggy waves that framed her eyes. Her reflection showed an older girl now—a teenager. Sassy loved it.

Sassy sat on the kitchen floor and untied her run-over oxfords. She peeled off her dirty socks, shorts, and shirt and threw them on the back porch, next to the washer.

"A young lady doesn't parade around in her underwear," Miss Dallas said. She flipped a rubber band around the finished book-lets. "I guess it's about time for you to start wearing that bra I bought you."

A blush of red rushed all the way down Sassy's chest. "I ain't wearing no slingshot," she said, but Sassy instinctively folded her arms over her budding breasts.

"Well, aren't you a little puzzle," Miss Dallas said. "All that talk about romance and love, but you're still acting like a stubborn tomboy. Don't you know boys like girls with a little figure?"

"Quit talking nasty!" Sassy found her dirty shirt on the floor and pulled it back over her head. "I'm going to take a bath."

"Wash that hair good."

Sassy ran down the hall and into the bathroom. She started the water in the tub and pulled off her shirt. She didn't need Miss Dallas to tell her boys liked girls with big chests. Sassy knew that from *Love Confessions*. Sassy took a breath of air and puffed out her chest until she was about sway-backed.

Sassy sat in the tub hugging her knees. Being born a girl was a big disappointment. As if getting a period and wearing a bra all day long wasn't bad enough, nice girls had to hold their tongues and behave. She couldn't tell Boon she liked him—that was forward. Heaven forbid if she were to ask Boon how he felt about her. It was rude. Nice girls were polite and proper, but the girls in *Love Confessions* never were and they always lived happily ever after. Miss Dallas didn't know what she was talking about.

Sassy finished bathing, washed her hair, and curled the edges under her fingers. Then, she found the bra at the bottom of her old toy box, where she had thrown it the minute Miss Dallas had brought it home. Sassy put it on and adjusted the straps. She found a cream-colored top sewn with a ruffle along the midriff and some clean shorts, and looked in the back of her closet for her Keds. She made one last check into the mirror and smiled. She cleaned up good.

By the time Sassy came back into the kitchen, it was lunchtime. Miss Dallas already had the sandwiches stacked on a platter in the center of the table and was pouring milk for Lula and Daddy.

"Well, aren't you the real McCoy?" Miss Dallas beamed at Sassy, and Sassy smiled back. She did feel pretty.

At the table, Lula had Daddy cornered in a one-way conversation about Elvis. Daddy never noticed Sassy, but he wasn't paying that much attention to Lula, either. He was preoccupied with his precious *Farm Report*.

Lula's gold mane was a smooth pageboy now. The short hair didn't hurt her looks one bit. "Elvis has more talent in his little finger than all The Beatles put together," she said. "Even the radio disc jockey said that Elvis had a better singing voice."

Lula loved Elvis. Last summer, she had read every single Elvis fan magazine from the Cheap Cash and had paid over five dollars in chore money to the official fan club for an authentic autographed photo of Elvis from the movie *Blue Hawaii*.

To Lula,
Aloha,
Elvis Presley
XXOO

Lula had added the hugs and kisses herself. She kept her prized picture in a gilded frame next to her bed. And to everyone in the household, it was hands off. Elvis belonged to Lula. "He's not just some rock'n'roll act," Lula said. "I swear his voice is a gift from God."

"You don't say," Daddy said.

"Don't you think he has a dreamy voice?"

Daddy didn't answer.

"Daddy!" Lula pouted.

"Sorry," he said. He glanced up and took a bite of his sandwich. "I'm listening, but I miss that ponytail of yours bobbing up and down when you talk. It's not the same."

"It'll grow out," Miss Dallas said. She sat a glass of milk down on the table.

Lula looked at her plate, mourning her lost mane. "My hair grows really fast," she said. But she gave Sassy a foul look and didn't say another word about his lordship Elvis.

Sassy daydreamed as she ate. Boon was telling her she was the most beautiful girl in Kentucky. Did she know she was so ravishing? Would she honor him with one small, tiny kiss? Would she marry him? Would she ... ?

"What?" Sassy didn't hear what Lula had said.

"How's your love life?" Lula repeated to Sassy.

Sassy bit into the bread crust. "I don't have a love life," she said.

"Just wondering," Lula said. "I put your ironing away this morning and saw a *Love Confessions* in your underwear drawer. What with clean clothes and that …" Lula reached over and snapped Sassy's bra strap. "I thought you might have a boyfriend we should know about."

Daddy's eyebrows shot up, and he looked over at Miss Dallas.

"Lula Thompkins, do you want to leave this table?" Miss Dallas warned.

"Just asking," Lula said. "Sassy's such a tomboy, I wondered why she's all cleaned up, that's all. I bet it's like one of those stories in her romance magazines. Sassy's in love!"

"Lula!" Daddy said.

Sassy threw a handful of potato chips, catching in Lula's hair. "What were you doing in my underwear anyway, Miss Nosy? I don't recall asking you to iron my panties."

"You still have some of those magazines, Sassy?" Daddy asked. "Thought I told you to get rid of them."

"I guess I forgot one was in there," Sassy said. Lula Willis Thompkins would be sorry she ever opened her mouth.

Daddy didn't say a word. His chair scraped back against the wood floor, and he disappeared down the hall. The sound of slamming drawers echoed in the quiet of the kitchen.

In a minute, Daddy reappeared and threw two *Love Confessions* in the kitchen trash, but not the issue with the love test. Sassy had hid it under her pillow that morning. "Don't let me catch you with these again," he said to Sassy. "They're nothing but a bunch of made-up stories."

"No they're not! They're true," Sassy argued.

"Like hell they are!" Daddy raised his voice, then stopped. "Don't say another word about it." He sat down and finished his sandwich in a fixed silence that filled the kitchen. Sassy gave Lula hateful stares across the table, but Lula never looked up.

"I got to go," Daddy said. "Some boys over the tobacco auction are looking for work."

"We'll get those magazines out to the burn barrel," Miss Dallas promised.

Daddy nodded and jingled his truck keys. "Those stories are just dreamed-up lies, Sassy. You are too young to read that garbage." The back screen door slammed against the house, and Daddy was gone.

Sassy could feel the burn of embarrassment spread over her face. Resentment rolled in her stomach, and she kicked Lula's leg under the table as hard as she could.

"Ouch! Sassy kicked me!"

"It was an accident," Sassy said. Her eyes narrowed into a hateful glare.

"Hush, both of you," Miss Dallas said. "Just eat."

Lula pulled the potato chips from her hair, and the girls finished lunch without speaking.

"Sassy, clean up the kitchen while Lula finishes the ironing," Miss Dallas said, clearing the table. "Your daddy said you owed me some household money for Cokes. Did you charge yourself something at the Cheap Cash?"

"I got a few things, but I got my baby-sitting money," she said. Sassy ran down the hall and found the envelope with the money, then hid the envelope back in its secret place. "Here you go."

"You didn't buy a new *Love Confessions*, did you?" Lula asked.

Sassy didn't answer her sister.

"What did you buy?" Miss Dallas folded the money and put it in her pocket.

"Nothing."

"Kind of an expensive nothing," Miss Dallas said.

"Two cherry Cokes and some female things. You want to go make a list of everything in my room so you can worry about it?"

"What female things?" Miss Dallas asked.

"Nothing. Why do you have to know every little thing I do? It's my money. Are you the warden all the sudden?"

"You bought *two* Cokes?" Lula asked.

"I was real thirsty," Sassy said.

"You were not," Lula said. "You bought a Coke for somebody. I'm going to ask Mr. Frankie."

"Girls!" Miss Dallas interrupted them. "Go on, and get your work done. I'm tired of your arguing."

Sassy cleared the rest of the table and ran water over the dishes in the sink. She could hear Elvis singing "Devil in Disguise" down the hall where Lula had a date with the ironing board. Even Elvis knew the truth about Lula.

Miss Dallas brought in dried towels from the clothesline and dropped the bundle on the table, half of it falling on the floor. She popped the towels in the air and folded them with the sureness of a drill sergeant.

"You bought a Coke for Boon Chisholm?" Miss Dallas asked. "That's what your daddy said."

"You told me to act like a young lady," Sassy said. "Mr. Frankie wouldn't give him credit. He acted worse than an old coot."

"Sassy!"

"I couldn't just drink my Coke standing right in front of Boon! That would be rude. He said he'd pay me back." Sassy stirred the plates in the hot soapy water. She wasn't about to mention the groceries.

"So he's not your boyfriend?" Miss Dallas halfway smiled. "You know that will be the story once Lula tells it."

"I can't help Lula's lies."

"Sassy, Boon is a lot older than you are, with a lot on his shoulders." Miss Dallas smoothed the towels stacked on the table. "That mother of his is nothing but a baby-making machine."

Sassy sloshed some dishwater onto the floor on purpose. She didn't answer.

"You better leave Boon alone." Miss Dallas hugged an armload of folded towels to her chest. "Your daddy finds you're boy-crazy, you'll be locked in your room for sure. Boon Chisholm won't bring you a thing but trouble."

"I don't need your advice about boyfriends," Sassy said. She didn't want to have this conversation. "I can take care of myself, thank you very much."

Miss Dallas tilted her head and tried to catch Sassy's glance. "Well, aren't you a little know-it-all?" she said. "I guess you got all the answers to those love questions?"

Sassy scooped up some soap bubbles and blew them at Miss Dallas. "No, but stop worrying about my love life. You're not my mama."

"I can only thank the Lord." The woman disappeared down the hall.

Miss Dallas could stop being a fusspot any old time. Besides, Boon didn't like her. But then, he hadn't seen her all dolled up with a new hairdo, either.

Sassy blew on a bubble from the dish soap and daydreamed about Boon. "Mrs. Boon Chisholm," she said to herself. "And they lived happily ever after."

12

WOW, WHERE DID YOU LEARN TO **KISS** LIKE THAT?" HE SAYS. "I GUESS I'M A NATURAL." JUST THEN I BECOME THE MOST POPULAR GIRL AT THE PARTY. I'VE ALWAYS HEARD BOYS LOVE FRENCH KISSING, AND I GUESS THEY DO.

Sassy finished the dishes but didn't want to stay in the house with Miss Dallas. She didn't want to listen to Lula's screeching, either. Lula sang loud and off-key to "Jailhouse Rock" until Sassy pounded on her sister's bedroom door and suggested Lula shut up before she called up every cat in Grayson County. Lula opened the door long enough to flick water on Sassy and threaten her with the hot iron until Sassy ran into the yard.

Sassy sat sidesaddle on the propane tank out front, and the silver steel of the tank burned into her skin. She swung her leg over and rode bareback.

Just before she got sick, Mama had taken a picture of Sassy and Lula riding the propane tank. Both girls were dressed like Annie Oakley. Sassy was barely a year old, so she didn't remember the picture being taken at all. But she remembered riding the tank with Lula. They were star trick riders and inseparable.

A swaying motion caught Sassy's attention

at the side of the house. She turned back and looked down toward the gate. No one was there. She slid off the tank, crouched down behind it, and listened: a few songbirds and the sound of a tractor mower off in a field somewhere, but something else, too—a peppered sound, like rain.

Sassy sneaked around by the front porch and made her way toward the side of the house. She peeked around the corner. It was Boon, standing behind a clump of honeysuckle. He tossed a handful of gravel over toward Lula's window.

Boon had come to see her?

"Hey!" Sassy said. She held her finger to her lips and whispered loud enough for Boon to hear. "That's not my bedroom. It's Lula's. She's going to come out here if you're not careful." Sassy waved for Boon to meet her out by the road.

He hesitated, then followed the honeysuckle underbrush away from the house. In a minute, he joined Sassy at the end of the driveway.

"It's okay. I don't think Lula heard a thing," Sassy said. She looked back at the house. Lula was probably serenading the ironing full blast, and Miss Dallas might be out back collecting laundry. They were safe.

"Your daddy here?" Boon asked.

"No," Sassy said. Disappointment caught her in the chest. "He went over to the tobacco auction to hire some men to help cut. I'll walk you over there if you want."

Boon smiled his million-dollar smile and seemed to relax a little. "Well, don't tell him I said hello," Boon said.

Sassy laughed.

"Where's Miss Dallas?" Boon said, looking toward the vegetable garden. "She back there annoying your sister?"

"I think it's the other way around," Sassy said. They walked down from the gate, out of sight of the yard.

"Now don't be talking ugly about your kin." Boon looked past Sassy toward the tobacco barn. "Shouldn't we walk down the road some more?"

Sassy checked again. "It's okay," she said. "Miss Dallas is out back hanging up clothes."

"While I'm here I guess I should take care of a little business," he said. Boon dug into his pocket. "Here's a payment on the groceries." He handed her a wad of change and a dollar bill.

"You don't have to pay me back," Sassy said. "I already gave Miss Dallas the money. I didn't say a thing. Daddy won't find out, I promise."

"Would you just take the money without arguing for once?" Boon waited for her to hold out her hand. "Please? With sugar on it? A man doesn't want to be in debt."

Sassy softened, opened her hand, and let coins and folded money drop into her palm. She jingled the coins in her hand, folded the dollar, and slipped the money in the pocket of her shorts. They stood in the road without talking for a minute.

"You cut your hair," Boon said.

Sassy pulled her bangs away from her brow. "I did it myself," she said. "Miss Dallas says it looks all grown up."

"She's right," Boon said.

Sassy grinned with pleasure. Again, a long moment of silence, while Sassy rubbed her Ked along the edge of the blacktop.

"I tore up that note," Sassy said. "From yesterday ..."

"Why did you run away?"

"'Cause you never said if you liked me," she said. "Figured I overstayed my welcome."

Boon glanced toward the house. "But I do like you, Sassy."

Sassy climbed up on the fence. "You do?"

"You don't know that?" An expression of mock surprise danced in Boon's eyes.

"I kind of wondered when I was chasing you with that cherry Coke." Sassy grinned down at Boon.

Boon shook his head. "I gave you a piece of gum! I don't do that with just anybody." Boon put his hands in his pockets and leaned against the fence.

Sassy could feel the heat of him standing so near. "So what exactly do you like about me?"

"What?" Boon looked back again at the house.

"You said you liked me just now," she said. "That's what you said. So tell me one thing you like about me."

"Did I say that?" Boon pulled up a milkweed and chewed on the raw grass. "Are you sure?"

"You sure as sure did," Sassy said. "You can't say something like that unless you mean it."

"You're not shy, are you?"

She didn't care if she was forward. "You said you liked me. I just wondered what all you liked."

"You said you wanted to know *one* thing," Boon corrected her.

"One thing out of everything." Sassy looked out into the tobacco, away from Boon. "Unless you are just a big old liar," she said. "Are you?"

Boon threw away the milkweed. "Well, there might be a thing or two I like about you."

Sassy waited while Boon pretended to think over his answer. "I like your new haircut!" he said.

Sassy jumped down from the fence. "Boon, if you want to be my steady boyfriend, then you better start sweet-talking me some."

"Wait! Wait. Wait. Wait. Wait. Boyfriend?"

"If you like me, don't you want to be my boyfriend?"

"But what—"

Sassy wouldn't let him finish his sentence. "Then just tell me I'm pretty. And how you would do anything in the world for me. And how you would just die if I moved away or something."

"I told you I liked you, but Sassy ..."

"You don't have to say it in front of people," Sassy said. "Are you too scared to be my boyfriend?" She goaded him a little.

"Too smart," Boon corrected her.

"But I thought you liked me," Sassy said.

"I do."

"Then you're my steady boyfriend, like it or not." Sassy looked at Boon.

His eyes narrowed, like he was figuring the odds. "I don't think you get to do the deciding, Sassy."

"Well, I ain't going to argue you into it. You said you liked me." Didn't Boon want to pull her gently to him, look deep into her eyes, and kiss her? That's how it always was in *Love Confessions*.

Boon scratched the back of his head and stood up from the fence. "I guess I am a boy. And I am your friend. That makes me your boy *friend*," Boon teased.

"No!" Sassy could feel the pounding of her own heartbeat just under her skin. "I mean girlfriend–boyfriend. You know what I mean." Sassy sighed.

Boon was playing with her now. How could she get his attention? Didn't he know she was serious? "You can kiss me," she said. "If you like me."

Boon blew air out his lungs in a long steady breath. "What are you talking about? What do you know about kissing?"

"Everything."

"No, you don't."

"I sure do!"

"You ever even been kissed?"

"I know how to French kiss," Sassy blurted out. She had read about it in *Love Confessions*.

"Sassy, don't be telling tales." Boon shook his finger at her, but the grin on his face told her Boon wasn't too upset. "You're flat-out lying."

"I'm not. I'll prove it right now." What was so tricky about French kissing anyway? You didn't need kissing school to stick your tongue down somebody's throat.

"I didn't know you were that kind of girl."

"What kind of girl?"

"A French-kissing girl," Boon said.

"I thought that was good."

"You gonna gossip to Lula and Miss Dallas?"

"I ain't no kiss and tell," Sassy said. She tilted her head, and her bra strap slid out from under her blouse. Dang Miss Dallas. What did a good-girl reputation matter if you ended up a wallflower in the shadow of a beautiful sister?

"I dare you to kiss me." Sassy grinned.

Boon hesitated, then leaned in and kissed her quickly on the cheek. "There, I kissed you."

She frowned.

"Sassy," Boon said in a low voice. He looked past her toward the house.

Sassy stepped toward him.

He didn't step away. "Good God, Sassy." A dry laugh stumbled from his throat.

Sassy grabbed his shirt, tiptoed as tall as she could, and kissed him with everything she had. His lips were soft against hers, and she pulled him closer to her. The faint smell of tobacco filtered through her nose, and she felt his hand on her back. Sassy pushed her tongue into his mouth, but he nudged her away, so she lingered on his lips one more moment before she pulled back and looked at him.

Boon hadn't looked at her that way before—surprised and curious, too. "Where did you learn to kiss like that?" he asked.

"Was it bad?"

"Terrible," Boon said. "Just terrible." He smiled.

Sassy ran her hand over her hair and looked down at the ground. She felt pretty.

"Guess I better get out of here," Boon said. "Might have to kiss you back if I stay." He laughed at his own joke.

"Boon? Do you really like me?"

"What's not to like?" he said.

"You want to be my boyfriend?"

He looked back toward the yard. "Do I have a choice?" He winked, stepped back into the uncut weeds by the road, and was gone.

But a shiver grabbed hold of Sassy. Boon was her boyfriend, but now what? Once Lula found out, so did Daddy.

13

That night, Sassy's insides twisted and turned all through supper. She picked at Miss Dallas's Italian spaghetti.

In her mind, she replayed every second of her conversation with Boon. She had kissed him, and he liked it. She knew he did. No boy would ever call her Fish Lips again.

Boon was her boyfriend. But how could she ever show off to Lula without Daddy finding out?

Halfway through the meal, Miss Dallas leaned over and felt Sassy's forehead, then went into the kitchen and got the thermometer to take her temperature. Normal. For once, Sassy was glad for the silence at the supper table, and she escaped into her bedroom even before Lula bellyached about dish-drying duty.

Sassy leafed through the pages of her lone issue of *Love Confessions*. The love test seemed silly now. It didn't matter that she didn't know Boon's favorite color or deepest secret. He would tell her.

HE WAS FROM THE WRONG SIDE OF THE TRACKS, SO WE AGREED TO HIDE OUR LOVE. BUT HOW COULD I PRETEND THAT HE WAS JUST ANOTHER BOY? (SOB!) HE WAS MY PERFECT BOYFRIEND.

"I'm leaving now!" Miss Dallas yelled from the kitchen. Daddy had already gone to a Methodist deacons' meeting, and Lula had "Viva Las Vegas" turned up too loud to hear anything else. Sassy didn't want to answer.

Within a minute, the woman tapped on Sassy's door and opened it just as Sassy slid the *Love Confessions* under her pillow. "I'm going home now," Miss Dallas repeated. "Close that window. It's raining."

Sassy didn't say anything.

"How you feeling?"

"I don't know how you figure I'm sick," Sassy said. She got up to pull the window sash down, but tiny flecks of rain had already dampened the curtains. "You can go on home."

"I will, then," Miss Dallas said. "Come lock the back door."

Sassy followed Miss Dallas out to the kitchen, and the woman collected her purse and a brown grocery bag of muskmelons from the vegetable garden. She stopped and looked at Sassy. "I saw Boon talking to you out front this afternoon. Don't think I don't know."

"Know what?"

"You a nervous Nellie all evening. You got boyfriend problems?"

"No! Boon came and paid me back for the Coke, that's all."

"I hope you're telling the truth," Miss Dallas said. "Sassy, good girls don't go chasing around after boys."

"You don't know anything about it," Sassy said.

"I know more than you think," Miss Dallas said. The woman slipped a clear plastic rain bonnet over her head and opened the back door. The smell of rain flooded the room. "You're in love with love," she said. "And it's going to get you in trouble."

"I thought you were going home," Sassy said.

"I am, Miss Smart Aleck. Lock the dead bolt. Your daddy might be late. Good night now."

Sassy turned the lock, wandered into the living room, and lay back on the worn-out divan. Shadowy streaks of rain patterned the wall where Mama and Daddy's wedding picture hung silent and still. Mama stood with Daddy in front of a big palm tree painted on a piece of canvas, a white gardenia in her hair. She wore a pink-tinted suit, and Daddy had on his United States Air Force uniform. They were smiling themselves silly.

A familiar loneliness fixed in Sassy's chest. There was nothing wrong about having Boon for a boyfriend. He liked her, and he smiled like some beautiful Hollywood movie star. Sassy's stomach prickled both excited and scared when she thought about him.

Sassy pulled out the tattered picture album she had made when she was nine. She ran her hand over the blue-checked binding, frayed into tiny strings that ran down the right side of the cover. She had looked at the pictures of Mama until she could see them clear as could be in her mind's eye. She didn't even need to turn on the light.

Mama's school picture when she was thirteen. Mama laughing in front of the Alamo on her honeymoon with Daddy. Pregnant by the back porch. With a newborn Lula outside the hospital.

There weren't any pictures of Mama and Sassy, but Sassy fancied she kind of looked like Mama around the mouth, with full lips and a square chin. In her heart, Sassy imagined she was like Mama in other ways, too, although she never knew one thing about Mama except from the once-in-a-blue-moon stories Daddy or Miss Dallas might tell. She outlined Mama's face with her finger and blinked hard.

Lula startled her. "Why are you sitting in the dark? Did Miss Dallas leave?" she asked. "It's about to storm. Turn on that lamp."

Lula fell on the divan next to Sassy and blew on the tips of her fingers. "I just painted my nails," she said. "What are you doing?"

"Nothing," Sassy said. "Looking at pictures."

Lula leaned over and squinted against the glare. "I hate those old pictures of Mama. We should just throw them away," she said. "Why do you stare at them all the time?"

"I don't."

"You do too." Lula pulled the album from Sassy's arms and tossed it on the floor.

"You remember much about Mama?" Sassy asked. "I can't remember nothing."

"I kind of remember her smell sometimes, for no reason. But that's all—thinking about her is depressing, so I don't do it." Lula blew on her nails.

Sassy picked up the album and flipped through it.

"Mr. Frankie said you bought a cherry Coke and a bunch of groceries for Boon Chisholm the other day," Lula said. "Female things, huh?"

"Boon paid me back, and I paid Miss Dallas." Sassy stared at the picture of Mama holding Lula. "Ain't nothing to tell."

"You better be careful fawning all over him. He's too old for you. You'll make a fool of yourself."

"I was just being a nice young lady." Sassy smiled a fake smile. "Mr. Frankie tell you he wouldn't give Boon any credit? Boon needed those groceries, so I helped out." Sassy changed the subject. "Was Mama sick a long time?"

"Why do you keep asking all this?" Lula said, blowing on her nails to dry them. "I was three years old. I don't know."

"Well, Daddy never says nothing. I just …"

"For the millionth time, Mama went to visit Granny Ellis, and she got real sick. Ate up with cancer, they said. Granny Ellis wanted us to come live with her, but Daddy didn't want us to.

And that's all. I'm not telling you again."

Poor Mama. Smiling like that on the outside and cancer eating her alive on the inside. Sassy closed the album and pulled some of the strings out from the cover.

Lula nudged Sassy's shoulder. "So, you got a little crush on Boon?" she asked. "Is that why you asked me about Elgin?"

"No!" Sassy said. She slipped the photo album back into the bookcase.

"I bet you do," Lula said. "Stealing around, trying to see …"

"Stop it," Sassy said.

"Mr. Frankie said he was going to tell Daddy."

"What did he say?" Sassy said.

"Said that you butted in to the conversation and acted like a little terror, screaming like a hellcat until he gave you the groceries. And that Boon flirted with you the whole time," Lula said. "Mr. Frankie called you a spoiled troublemaker."

"He's the troublemaker."

"You better stay away from Boon. He's not going to like you."

"Why don't you mind your own business?" Sassy's voice got loud. "Mr. Frankie loves making mountains out of molehills."

"I think he's got himself a mountain this time," Lula said. "And Daddy will want to know all about it."

"He won't care." But Sassy knew he would.

"He will too. Daddy will know you lied, and your bottom will burn right along with those romance magazines."

"Thanks to you and Mr. Frankie gossiping about nothing."

"Boon's not some Romeo out of your dumb love stories. You're in over your head, and Daddy's going to hit the ceiling. You are such an idgit."

It was all Sassy could do to keep from telling Little Miss Lula-Know-It-All that she could just shut up. Boon was her boyfriend. He liked her. He liked her kiss.

But Sassy didn't say anything. She was already out of the living room and halfway down the hall. Sassy slammed her bedroom door so hard that the windows on that side of the house vibrated as if a tiny earthquake had rumbled deep in the earth. Lula was determined to tell Daddy, and Sassy had to talk to Mr. Frankie before he had a chance to stir things up even more.

Lightning illuminated Sassy's bedroom, followed by a bellow of distant thunder. The lights flickered dim, then went black. There was nothing she could do until morning. Well, maybe there was one thing. Lula was terrified of the dark.

14

Sassy crossed the street to the Cheap Cash under a clear sky. The storm had kept the lights off for more than an hour last night, long enough for Sassy to make scraping sounds on the back porch and wait for Lula to call out in terror. Lula almost cried she was so scared and insisted they both hide in her closet.

When Sassy burst out laughing, Lula pushed her out into the hall and locked her bedroom door. Sassy sat in the hall for a good ten minutes calling for Lula to help her, while her sister yelled threats at her. When the lights came on, Sassy stayed up until Daddy got home to make sure Lula didn't go tattling any tales about Boon.

Sassy jumped over the muddy ditch across the street from the Cheap Cash and practiced her speech to Mr. Frankie. She wouldn't mind eating a whole humble pie if it kept the old man from talking to Daddy.

Dang Lula. Sassy couldn't wait to tell Lula that Boon was her real-deal boyfriend. But first, she had to get things worked out with Daddy.

IT'S A FAIR TRADE. I WANT A HOME, AND HE NEEDS SOMEONE TO TAKE CARE OF HIM. PEOPLE GET MARRIED FOR LESS. NO USE GETTING ALL EMOTIONAL ABOUT IT. IT'S ONLY **LOVE.**

Sassy pushed her hair back from her forehead and mustered up her courage. She jiggled the front door. Mr. Frankie was behind the counter, talking to Boon's mama. Mrs. Chisholm was all dressed up in a flowered sundress and high heels and carrying a tiny patent-leather purse.

"Hello," Sassy said. She felt as if she had interrupted them.

Mr. Frankie waved his hand at her. "I don't have any cherry Cokes today. All sold out." Mr. Frankie sure wasn't about to forgive and forget.

"Why, it's that angel Sassy Thompkins," Mrs. Chisholm said. "Walter here was just telling me about the groceries, and how nice you were to Boon." She pulled a bright pink lipstick out of her purse and used the mirror behind the soda fountain to fix her face.

Mr. Frankie didn't take his eyes off Sassy. "Don't think I called you an angel," he said. "Sugar, heaven would be hell with you screaming all the time."

Mrs. Chisholm ignored Mr. Frankie's comment. "I guess our little business is all concluded, Walter? Can you deliver everything on my grocery list today?" Mrs. Chisholm smoothed her hair and winked into the mirror.

Mr. Frankie nodded and came around the counter.

Mrs. Chisholm stood close to him. From the look on his face, he didn't mind one bit. "I'll be home all afternoon," she said.

Sassy shifted her weight and rubbed one of her Keds on the back of her leg. Was Mr. Frankie set to be husband number five?

Mrs. Chisholm snapped her purse and smiled down at Sassy. "I like your new haircut," she said. "It's darling."

Sassy just stared; she didn't know what to say.

"Tootle-loo," Mrs. Chisholm said. "See you later, Walter." She gushed out charm like an overflowing Coca-Cola.

Sassy and Mr. Frankie eyed each other for a moment. An uncomfortable weak feeling crept around Sassy's stomach. She shifted her weight from one foot to the other.

"What do you want?" he asked.

Sassy didn't look up. "I'm here to apologize," she said. "I was disrespectful screaming and all, and I'm sorry."

The old man's eyes narrowed. "So you're sorry now?" He fumbled through junk on a shelf behind him to find a flyswatter. A fly buzzed around the cash register.

"Yes, sir," Sassy said. "A little birdie told me you were all riled up and …" She chewed the inside of her cheek.

"And you didn't want your daddy hearing about it? Well, I hope Lula talked some sense into you."

The fly landed on the counter and Mr. Frankie snapped the swatter in a perfect slap. "Boon Chisholm was already pushing his weight around pretty good, and you jumped right in."

"Miss Dallas is after me to be a nice young lady, and that's what I tried to do," Sassy said. "Boon paid me back."

"And I guess you gave that money to your daddy?"

"I took care of it. Why does it matter to you anyway?"

"I got a responsibility to this town. You're nothing but a little girl, and you played right up to Boon like some floozy. You're going to get a reputation you won't like, young lady. " He waved the flyswatter toward Sassy.

"I didn't do anything wrong."

"Well, if you were acting decent, your sister wouldn't come over here trying to keep you out of trouble."

"Lula's just trying to stir up something."

"She was worried sick. Boon told her you been chasing after him all over town."

"She's a liar! That's not true."

Mr. Frankie's face turned gray. "Well, you sure played into

him the other day. Lula said you were out of control, and, sugar, she was right."

"Lula needs her mouth washed out with soap," Sassy said. She hesitated. "I guess you're going to bend Daddy's ear out of meanness?"

"I sure am. Soon as he comes in here," Mr. Frankie said. "Somebody needs to rein you in, little girl."

"What about you?"

"Don't start with me!"

Sassy had a mind to slap every jar on the counter right onto the floor.

"You gossiped with Lula like y'all were a couple of hens!"

"Get out of here!" Mr. Frankie batted the flyswatter at Sassy.

"I'm taking back my apology!" Sassy yelled. "You don't deserve it!" She turned and protest-marched out the door.

Lula had lied about Boon. He never said Sassy was chasing him all over town. He wouldn't say that. Lula never even talked to Boon. She was a little snot who was too good to talk to anybody—unless she wanted something.

There was nothing else to do but to come clean with Daddy about the groceries. That would fix Lula. Daddy would drag Lula right down to the Cheap Cash and make her admit the truth to Mr. Frankie before nightfall. Sassy would skip the part about Boon being her boyfriend, of course. She would break that news to Daddy in about a million years.

Boon was right. Mr. Frankie was a jackass. Why would Mrs. Chisholm want him for a husband? The thought of kissing an old man like him made her want to puke.

Sassy hurried home to find Daddy. Lula would be sorry she started this whole thing. Daddy might get mad, but the truth would cook Lula's goose good.

15

Sassy found Daddy at the tobacco barn repairing a section of rafter.

"Sassy, get back now. These beams are heavy," Daddy said. A bulky rope held the rafter beam in place. Lines of sunlight poured through the slits of the ventilation shutters and hid Daddy's face in shadow.

"I need to talk to you, Daddy." Sassy's breath was uneven. She had run the full distance from the Cheap Cash. Lula would get the whipping of her life once Daddy heard all about her lies. "It can't wait."

"What can't wait?"

Sassy yelled in between hammer blows. "I got to tell you something, Daddy. Please."

The banging stopped and Daddy climbed down the ladder. "What is it? Where are Miss Dallas and your sister?"

"I don't know … at home, I guess."

Daddy flipped his hat back and wiped the sweat from his forehead. "So what's the emergency?" he asked.

NOBODY GETS JAILED FOR BREAKING HEARTS. NO ONE EVEN GETS A PARKING TICKET. BUT THAT DOESN'T MEAN YOU HAVE TO BE CUPID'S VICTIM. YOU CAN THROW LOVE A PUNCH OR TWO OF YOUR OWN.

"The other day Miss Dallas said I should quit acting like a tomboy and start being a young lady."

"Okay."

"And I didn't know what she meant, but I did too, kind of. So when I went to the Cheap Cash the other day and bought myself that cherry Coke, Boon came in, but Mr. Frankie wouldn't give him no credit when he tried to buy groceries."

"And?"

"And I couldn't just drink my Coke in front of Boon. That wouldn't be nice, so I bought him a Coke. But then—with Miss Dallas's advice and all—I decided to buy Boon's groceries, too, only Mr. Frankie didn't like it."

"What did he say to you?"

"Said it was none of my business, but he treated Boon like dirt, Daddy."

"That's none of your concern."

"But he was mean, and Boon needed those groceries."

"Did Boon pay you back?"

"Yes, sir, came by yesterday afternoon and gave me some money."

"And you lied to me about buying female things?"

"I thought you'd be real mad at me."

"Sassy, I don't want you involved with Mr. Frankie's business. What's this all about? I'm busy."

Sassy chewed the inside of her lip. "Lula."

Daddy's eyebrows went up. "What in a hill of beans does your sister have to do with all this?"

"She went and stuck her nose into everything and said a bunch of lies to Mr. Frankie about me chasing after Boon, and now Mr. Frankie is worse than an old dog about it."

"Sassy!"

"Well, he is! He said I acted like a floozy."

"What the hell did you do to provoke that?"

"Nothing! I swear, nothing, Daddy! I went over this morning to tell him I was sorry, and he got all mad at me."

"Sorry for what?"

Sassy hesitated. "I was rude. Told him it was none of his concern how I spent my baby-sitting money. Said the cherry Cokes in Leitchfield were better."

"Dag gum it, Sassy!"

"Mr. Frankie wouldn't sell me the groceries for Boon 'cause I didn't have your permission to put them on our account." Sassy's voice got quiet. Maybe Daddy wouldn't hear. "So I had a screaming fit until he gave up. ..."

"You what?"

"Well, I said I went over to apologize!"

"Sassy, how old are you?"

"Eleven. Twelve, October second."

"You're old enough to know better than to go over to the Cheap Cash and stir up things with Mr. Frankie. You know he gets on something and won't let it be."

"But Daddy, I didn't stir up things! It was Lula! She's the one that lied! I'm not tattling—I'm just repeating what she said."

"So you're blaming your sister?"

"I was just being nice, like Miss Dallas said to do. And that old man twisted everything up, thanks to Lula." Sassy's voice broke. "I'd make Lula go over there and tell Mr. Frankie the truth is what I'd do. Then, I'd tan Lula's hide if I was you."

"You would?"

"She deserves it."

Daddy's gaze was hard. "You got a crush on that boy?"

"I just said I was being nice. That's all I was doing, honest."

"Then stay away from Boon Chisholm and out of the Cheap Cash and that will solve your problem."

"But Daddy ... Lula ..."

"Sassy, you heard what I said, and I'm as serious as a heart attack about this—mind me, or you're the one who's going to be in trouble."

"I didn't do anything!"

"Sassy!" Daddy said. "You're a little girl pushing up against things you don't know about. The Chisholms are wilder than a bunch of coyotes, and Boon's mama don't pay them one bit of mind. They're not our kind. I know that sounds ugly, but it's true."

"But ... ," Sassy said.

"I got to go back to work," Daddy said. "Tobacco cutting is next week, and I can't be jawing around with you. Stay clear of Boon Chisholm; that's it. Do you hear me?"

Sassy didn't answer.

"Do you hear me?" Daddy said louder.

"Yes, sir," she said. "What about Lula?"

"I'll talk to her, but you don't need to go prattling around and making demands about your sister," Daddy said. "Go on in the house. Miss Dallas is probably looking for you."

Sassy watched Daddy climb back up the ladder, then she walked down the path and leaned against the propane tank. The sun was hot on her back. Daddy wasn't going to do a thing to punish Lula. Not one dang thing. Lula did whatever she pleased.

If Daddy wouldn't make Lula tell the truth, then Sassy would just have to do it herself.

16

"Lula!" Sassy's voice rang out empty, and the house creaked in the quiet. "Lula!" No answer. Sassy padded the back hallway toward Lula's room.

"Luulaa," she whispered into the door-frame. Sassy put her ear close to the door and her whole body froze to listen. No sound.

The perfumed air of Lula's bedroom was thick, and Sassy's breath slowed to a false calm. She walked straight to the *Blue Hawaii* photograph in its gold frame. Since Lula was in love with Elvis, she would do just about anything if her pride-and-joy picture of him disappeared all of a sudden. She would probably take her medicine and tell the truth to Mr. Frankie and to Daddy. That is, if Lula ever intended to see pretty boy Elvis again.

The back door screen thwacked loud against the still house, and Sassy jumped. The picture fell from her hands in a soft thud on the rug. She scrambled to pick it up, but a white envelope under the bed caught Sassy's glance. Boon's full

I WAS SUCH A FOOL. WHEN OUR FRIENDS TOLD ME TO WATCH OUT FOR HER, I DIDN'T PAY THEM ANY MIND. HE LOVED ME. I DIDN'T KNOW HOW MUCH LOVE COULD HURT, BUT I DO NOW. I'M NOT A VENGEFUL PERSON, BUT I COULD BE. I MIGHT BE.

name was written along the edge in a curlicue script.

"Sassy?" Miss Dallas yelled from the kitchen. "Are you home?"

Sassy grabbed the letter and Elvis and ran into the bathroom. She heard Miss Dallas's shoes slap the wooden floor of the hall.

"Hello? Hello? Sassy?"

Sassy locked the door and slid down the wall. She stared at the envelope. It was a letter addressed to Lula at church camp, but someone had written Boon's name all around the edge of the envelope in bright red ink. The handwriting belonged to Lula.

Sassy pulled out the letter—a single sheet of tablet paper.

Lula,
Miss you baby. Counting the days 'til you're home.
Boon

Sassy's heart almost stopped. Boon missed Lula? How … ? Why … ? She looked at the envelope again. It was postmarked three weeks ago from Falls of Rough, just before Sassy had come home from church camp—just before the spin-the-bottle incident.

Boon missed Lula. Her pretty sister with the gold hair. Boon with the Hollywood smile. The truth ripped raw into Sassy's lungs, and she gasped hard to breathe.

"Sassy?" Miss Dallas knocked on the door. "You in there?"

Sassy swallowed hard. "I'm trying to pee!" she yelled. Why else would Lula keep badgering her? Why else would Lula lie to Mr. Frankie? Boon was Lula's secret love. Sassy turned the envelope upside down. A chewing gum wrapper fell onto the floor. Tiny letters were written on the back.

Across from the bow bridge—tomorrow morning at 10.

Is that why Boon came to the house yesterday? To see Lula? There was no mistake at all—he knew which window was Lula's. He wanted Lula, not her.

Sassy's pulse beat fast and unfamiliar. She wadded the letter into a tight ball and threw it against the bathroom wall with all her strength, then ripped the gum wrapper into tiny bits, littering the bathroom. In anger, she backhanded a long, low shelf that contained Lula's special-blend bottle of Breck shampoo, her hairbrush, and a yellow aerosol bottle of Jean Naté cologne. The bottles shattered on the linoleum floor, and Lula's hairbrush floated in the toilet.

"Sassy, what's going on?" Miss Dallas said. "Did you break something?"

"I sure did!" she shrieked. Sassy hurled Elvis's picture into the bathtub.

"Open this door right now!" Miss Dallas jiggled the handle. "I'm going to knock it down if you don't."

"Go ahead!" Sassy yelped. Elvis stared back at Sassy. She grabbed up the picture frame and slammed it against the tiled edge of the bathtub. The glass cut inside the frame, and a long scratch sliced through Elvis's cheek. Sassy snatched up Lula's nail polish and poured it over Elvis's face. The Xs and Os smeared beneath the glass in a slow-moving goo of ink and paint. Sassy threw the frame into the toilet, next to the hairbrush. "Sassy Thompkins! Open this door!" The door grunted against Miss Dallas's weight. "Open it right now!"

"Go away!"

Boon had played with Sassy like a toy. He had made her believe he was her boyfriend, but all along he loved Lula. How could she have been so stupid? Boys ran around on girls in *Love Confessions* stories all the time. She should have known. She had read them all.

A sob came up into Sassy's throat, bitter and stinging. She bent over the sink and turned on the water to keep Miss Dallas from hearing her cry. Pain hung low in her stomach. Lula would always be the pretty sister with a thousand boyfriends. And now she had Boon, too. Sassy leaned over the sink and let the tears come.

Miss Dallas started to bang at the hinge pins with a hammer and a screwdriver. "Sassy, let me in! Please to God, open this door!"

Sassy ignored her. The constant pounding of Miss Dallas's hammer sent a pain behind her eyes. She hiccupped through her tears, splashed water on her face, and rubbed a towel across the tender skin of her nose. She hated Lula. And she hated Boon.

Across from the bow bridge ...

Sassy knew exactly where they were. Daddy wouldn't mind Sassy tattling now. She scrounged on the floor to find Boon's love note. She flattened out the paper, then smoothed it across her knee. Daddy could see for himself what a deceitful, lying daughter Lula Willis Thompkins was. Lula's little secret love was about to blow up in her pretty face.

"I'm coming in there, Sassy!" Miss Dallas still hammered. "It's going to be okay! I'm coming."

Sassy waited for the pop of the hammer to cover the sound of the bathroom window rising. She threw the screen onto the grass, stood on the toilet, and climbed out the window just before Miss Dallas gave a solid hammer blow to the last hinge and pulled the bathroom door from its frame.

All Miss Dallas found was broken glass, a disfigured picture of Elvis, and a hairbrush stopping up the toilet. Sassy was already halfway to the tobacco barn to find Daddy.

17

"Down here, Daddy," Sassy whispered, motioning to the narrow trail at the edge of the river. Sassy had run on ahead, but not by much.

Maybe Daddy would catch Lula and Boon red-handed. Sassy stepped quietly through the weeds, and Daddy followed. He seemed more worried than angry. Why wasn't he hopping-mad furious?

Sassy's footing slipped on the narrow ridge, past a hackberry bush. She bit her lip to keep from calling out, then dodged around a tree root and a large jog of rock. She scouted the riverbank below.

There they were. Through the wild scramble of branches Sassy saw them: the lovebirds. Boon had his arm around Lula's waist. The dog was kissing her. A sharp sting burned through Sassy's chest. It was Lula. It was always Lula.

Sassy ran down the embankment before Daddy could catch her and shoved Lula hard into Boon. Lula fell to her knees and let out a

A LYING DOG IS STILL A **LYING** DOG. EVEN WHEN HE'S SMILING AND WAGGING HIS TAIL. THE SAME IS TRUE IN **LOVE.**

whelp like the wind had been knocked out of her. Sassy punched at Boon. "Come on and fight me!" she yelled. "You scared to fight a girl, you lying Romeo?"

Boon grabbed her wrists and let her hands flail into the air. She kicked at his shins until he crossed her arms, spun her around, and held her tight against his side. She didn't let up. "You never had one bit of raising, Boon Chisholm! You been cheating on me from the start! You said you were my boyfriend!"

Lula stumbled to her feet. "Boon never liked you, Sassy! You were the one chasing him!"

Sassy thrust her foot at Lula. "That is not true!"

"It is too! You bought him those groceries and threw yourself right at him. Mr. Frankie told me!"

"Hush up, the both of you!" Daddy yelled. He jerked Lula's arm and she staggered sideways, dangling against his frame like a worn-out baby doll. "What the hell's going on here?"

"Sassy started it!" Lula shouted.

"I did not!" Sassy yelled. "I didn't know Boon was your stupid boyfriend. You sure didn't act like it at church camp when you played spin the bottle with Reeves Hanvey."

"You played, too!" Lula said. "You begged me to go along to the boys' cabin! You're the one who kissed Reeves."

Sassy stomped solid on Boon's foot.

"Why you little …" Boon let go long enough for Sassy to spin around and elbow him hard right in the mouth. Boon pushed her aside and cupped his jaw in his hand. "Son of a … ," he yelled.

"Sassy!" Daddy's voice roared out into the fray. "Get over here!" From the sound of his voice, Sassy knew Daddy meant business.

Boon bent over and spit blood on the ground. "You broke my tooth," Boon mumbled. He opened his hand to show a sliver of white enamel in a bloody palm. "And cut my lip. Thanks a lot."

A pink film covered his Hollywood smile, and the corner of his front tooth was missing.

"What's going on between you and my daughters?"

"Nothing now," Boon said. He pressed his fingers against his lip.

Sassy started to speak, but Daddy's glance told her to shut up.

"I swear 'fore to God, you're nearly a man, and you're playing around with my girls?" Daddy asked.

Lula interrupted. "We didn't do nothing wrong, Daddy. Boon's in love with me, and I am with him. Sassy made up everything about Boon being her boyfriend. She's dreaming. ..."

"Boon *said* he was my boyfriend!" Sassy corrected Lula. "He told me!"

"You dreamed that up from your silly romance magazines," Lula said. "You've been after him ever since you got home from church camp."

"He's the one that flirted. He talked to me and gave me chewing gum and said he liked me." Sassy saw the anger in Daddy's eyes. "I didn't know what to do, Daddy. I wasn't chasing Boon, I promise."

"You sure were! You kissed him!" Lula spit the words at her.

"Only after he said he liked me! He lied to me! He's nothing but a no-count liar."

"Stop it! Hush up, both of you!" Daddy's words had a hard edge. "You were both sneaking around with this boy behind my back?"

"It's not like that, Daddy," Lula said. "It was Sassy. She's the one that's got a crush on Boon and threw herself at him." Tears collected around Lula's eyes. "Boon loves me, and Sassy's ruined everything."

"Don't blame your sister for your own doing!" Daddy yelled

at Lula, then turned to Boon. "What do you have to say for yourself?"

Boon wiped his mouth with the back of his hand. "What do you want?" Boon said. "Nothing bad happened. I gave them both a little attention. What's wrong with that?"

Lula screamed at Boon. "I thought you loved me!"

Boon didn't answer.

"Love!" Daddy shouted. "What the hell do you know about love? God in heaven, Lula, you're not even fifteen! Do you think love is sneaking around and lying behind my back with some arrogant, smart-mouthed boy while he's flirting with your sister?"

Lula sobbed even more. "But Daddy, I love …"

"Don't say that! Don't you dare say that!"

Lula fell to the ground in tears.

Sassy yelled at Boon. "All the time you were palling around with Lula, you teased me and acted like you liked me! You never let on one thing!"

"How could I?" Boon said. He dabbed the cut again with his finger. "You didn't want to hear it! You were hell-bent on having a boyfriend, and nothing was going to stop you."

"You said you liked me!"

"You're one hell of a kisser, Sassy. I'm just not attracted to you," Boon said. "But you're going to make some man really happy someday."

"You lied to both of us," Sassy said.

"We all had fun."

"You hurt Lula, and you hurt me," Sassy said. "You don't care about anybody, do you?"

Sassy turned her back away from Boon—she wouldn't give him the satisfaction of seeing tears in her eyes. How could she have been so wrong? Nothing in *Love Confessions* could help her now.

Daddy pointed at Boon and spoke in a low tone that scared Sassy. "Stay away from my girls," he said. "You are nothing but lowlife scum, and they don't want any part of you."

"I don't want any trouble, but you don't know anything about me," Boon said. "I gave *your girls* exactly what they wanted. Neither one of them acted like they hated it." But Boon didn't stay to argue; he ran up the ravine and was gone.

Daddy grabbed Sassy's arm and pulled her and Lula up the path to the truck. "I tried to raise you girls decent. And this is what I get?"

Daddy opened the door and pushed Sassy and Lula into the cab. There was nothing pretty about her sister now. Lula's face was twisted red from crying.

"We didn't know Boon was playing with us, Daddy," Sassy said. "I didn't know Lula liked him. I thought he liked ..."

"Don't blame Boon in this. You're both as bad as he is. You both flat-out lied and conned me into thinking you were good girls, but it's all a show, isn't it?"

"We're good girls, Daddy," Lula's voice was small and trembling.

"Good girls don't sneak around with boys! They don't lie straight to my face. They don't end up in the boys' cabin playing spin the bottle at church camp. They don't fall in love with neighborhood trash and sneak behind my back. God knows what you've been doing."

Daddy turned over the engine and slammed the truck into reverse. "I work like a dog to make a good life for you girls, and you don't want it. Damn you both, you're just like your mother."

"You adored Mama," Sassy said.

Daddy laughed. "Yes I did!" he said. "And she made my life a living hell."

Sassy looked at Lula. Lula seemed startled, like some pent-up animal, scared of what Daddy might say. She grabbed hold of Sassy's hand and held it tight, as if to keep Sassy from falling off the edge of the earth.

"Your mother was a lying tramp," Daddy said. "She ran off to California a year after you were born, Sassy, and I haven't heard from her since. All she wanted was to run around behind my back. I guess both you girls come by it honest."

Sassy sat very still. A dead ache wrapped around her, and the loneliness in her heart billowed up in shame and disbelief. She didn't want to hear any more.

"I tried to protect you girls all these years. Figured if I loved y'all enough, then maybe, maybe ..." Daddy stopped. "Maybe I don't know what." His voice turned to a sarcastic sting. "So you girls could grow up and be happy ..." Daddy spun the tires in the dirt. "To hell with love. To hell with all of it."

Grief and fear and panic mixed up inside Sassy. The tears came uncontrollable. Mama was alive? She didn't love them? Lula held on to her and rocked her back and forth, but Lula wasn't crying at all now. She was dry-eyed and frozen.

When they got home, Miss Dallas came out on the porch, but Sassy ran past her without even looking up.

Mama didn't love them. And now Daddy didn't, either. Sassy collapsed on her bed, a burning hurt filling what was left of her heart. She jerked the *Love Confessions* from under her pillow and threw it into the trash can. She didn't want to know another thing about love. She knew too much already.

18

"Sassy? Sassy? It's Miss Dallas, honey."

Sassy didn't move. She lay on her side with her knees pulled up to her chin. A blank stare had replaced her tears hours ago. Out the window, the sun skimmed the edge of the horizon. Mama was alive out there somewhere.

"Sassy, let me talk to you." Miss Dallas opened the door, and the shade flapped against the window's breeze. "Your daddy told me what happened," she said. "Told me about Lula and Boon Chisholm. And you, too."

Sassy was quiet for a long time. "Did you know about Mama?"

"I did."

"Why didn't you say something to us?"

"It wasn't my secret to tell. Your daddy didn't want y'all to know, and I couldn't cross him." Miss Dallas sat down on the bed and waited.

"Mama looks happy in all those pictures we got in the living room," Sassy said. "Happy as a lark. You think she was pretending? You think she loved us any at all?"

MY HUSBAND BELIEVES **LOVE** IS BEDROCK. I SAY IT'S SHALE. BOTH LEAVE **SCARS.** I HAVE THE SKINNED KNEES TO PROVE IT.

"I don't know," Miss Dallas said. "But you can't tell, Sassy. She might have been sick in her mind or upset or scared about being a mama. We don't know how things were for her on the inside."

Sassy held her breath for a minute. She was afraid all the hurt would come rushing up into her throat.

"Sassy, when people fall in love, things can sort of get out of hand," Miss Dallas said. "It don't always go like you think."

"How do you know? You got some long-lost daughters somewhere?"

Miss Dallas let out a long sigh. "I know you're upset, Sassy, but …"

"I'm not upset."

"Okay."

Sassy blinked hard. "You think Daddy was mean to her?"

"I don't think so."

"She just stopped loving us, then."

"You don't know that." Miss Dallas smoothed Sassy's hair away from her face. "And the truth is you're probably never going to know. Your daddy don't know. She probably don't even know. Love is not like those stories in your magazine, honey. Sometimes there's not a happy ending."

Sassy turned to look at Miss Dallas. "Is that what happened to you?"

"What?"

"You said you was in love a long time ago. Did you just fall out of love?"

"I never said I was in love a long time ago."

"You did too!"

"I did not! I said I was in love one time. I didn't say when."

"So you in love now?"

Miss Dallas almost smiled "I don't know," she said. "Everything's kind of upside down."

"Does he love you?"

"Probably not like what you're thinking."

"How long you been waiting?"

"A while, but I'm not going anywhere."

Sassy sighed deep and pushed her pillow behind her head. "So, you going to wait till kingdom comes for somebody to love?"

"What makes you think I don't have someone to love? I love you and Lula. I wouldn't come here every day if I didn't love y'all."

"I guess that's good 'cause Daddy don't love me and Lula anymore," Sassy said. "*Through with love.* Said so hisself."

"Well, I don't believe that," Miss Dallas said. "Give him a little time. He loved your mama, and he got hurt bad. But hurts heal, Sassy. Love comes back around. It don't stay gone."

"Tell that to Daddy."

Miss Dallas stared at Sassy, but her face was kind and patient. "Now, what you going to do about Boon?"

Sassy pulled away. "Ask Lula. He's her boyfriend."

"I tried talking to her, but she's got the dresser pushed up against the door and won't answer."

Sassy's breath came quicker. "All I know is Boon Chisholm said he liked me. Smiled his Hollywood smile with those sugar-white teeth …" Sassy thought she might start crying again. "But he never liked me at all. He lied."

"Did he? Or did you just hear what you wanted to hear?"

"What do you mean?"

"Read things into it? Make more of it than you should have?"

"No! It was all his fault."

"You sure you didn't run after him?" Miss Dallas glanced at Sassy. "Even a little?"

"I might have run into him accidentally."

"Did you ever kiss him?"

"Maybe."

"Sassy?"

"No! Yes! He said I was a good kisser." Sassy stopped up short.

Miss Dallas didn't say anything. The quiet of the house gnawed on Sassy's nerves. She turned on her side and couldn't look at Miss Dallas anymore.

"I wanted somebody to love me," Sassy said. Her voice quivered into a whisper. "Love me more than anything on this earth. Like Mama. Like in the romance magazines. But it's all made-up."

"I don't know." Miss Dallas pulled Sassy into her lap. "Maybe you misunderstood 'cause you wanted something real bad, but people still fall in love all the time. It takes two to tango, that's all. Boon got caught up in his own opinion of himself. I don't think he meant to hurt y'all."

"I saw his mama," Sassy said. "She was with Mr. Frankie at the Cheap Cash."

"What do you mean?"

"Mrs. Chisholm's got her sights on Mr. Frankie being husband number five, I guess." Sassy picked at the bedspread; she didn't want to look at Miss Dallas.

"My word! Well, at least those kids will have some decent food."

"Lula can have Boon," Sassy said.

"She better stay away from him. I know she's got her heart broke, but Boon's not for her. She'll grow up a little and find someone else."

"Do you think Lula hates me?"

"Not at all. Why don't you talk to her? Maybe this will let you girls mend some fences. Stop all this fighting."

Sassy thought about it and nodded. She sat up and blew her nose into a rumpled Kleenex. "Do you think Daddy still loves us?"

"More than his own life," Miss Dallas said. "Why else would he make up that story for all these years? He didn't want you to be hurt by what your mama did. And that's why he was so mad when he caught you reading those love magazines. He didn't want you running around after something. …"

"You think Daddy wishes he had never met Mama?"

"Now why would he wish that? He was crazy in love with her."

"I bet he wishes he never had kids."

"Not a day. Y'all are his whole life. You're everything." Miss Dallas pulled the hair away from Sassy's eyes. "Besides, if he didn't have y'all, what would I do all day?"

Sassy started to grin. "Ever wished you had babies?" she asked.

"Heavens no!"

Sassy frowned. "Well, you could have wished a little."

A halfway smile came across Miss Dallas's face. "Maybe I did a long time ago, but now … I got what I want."

"You might have made a good mama." Sassy gave Miss Dallas a hard look. "You know, with a little more practice, you might still turn out."

Miss Dallas smiled wide. "Thank you," she said. "I appreciate the encouragement." Miss Dallas hugged Sassy close. And for just a minute, Sassy didn't hurt anymore. For just a minute, she didn't miss Mama.

19

> MY ADVICE IS TO GET THAT **FIRST LOVE** RIGHT OUT OF THE WAY. GO AHEAD AND JUMP IN HEAD OVER HEELS, BUT **END IT** THE FIRST EXCUSE YOU GET. THE REAL STUFF COMES LATER—WITH EXPERIENCE.

"Get up, Sassy!" Miss Dallas flipped the blanket off the bed. "Lula's gone!"

"What?"

"She's gone. Your daddy had a meeting at the new co-op in Leitchfield. I got here early this morning. She's not here. I've looked everywhere. Why in the world would she want to run off with that boy?"

Sassy pulled a pair of shorts off the chair and put them on over her shorty pajamas. "Did she leave a note?"

"No. But where else could she be? She barricaded herself in her room and cried all night. She's got to be with Boon. I've got to try and get hold of your daddy."

Sassy followed Miss Dallas into the kitchen. "You think they're over the Chisholms'?"

"I don't know, but I'd bet my eyeteeth that Boon's mama knows where they are."

Sassy rubbed her eyes and tried to think. Miss Dallas got out the telephone book.

"Do you remember the name of that man who runs the co-op?"

Sassy shook her head. She didn't.

"I'm going to have to drive over there, then." Miss Dallas fumbled through her purse for the keys. "Stay here in case Lula calls or comes home. I'll go get your daddy, and we'll head directly over to the Chisholms'. Maybe they haven't gone too far."

Sassy rubbed her hair back flat against her head. She was awake now. "Boon never said he loved Lula once yesterday. Do you think he's just trying to spite Daddy?"

"I have no idea." Miss Dallas grabbed her car keys. "I won't let anything happen. I'll talk to your daddy," she said, but Sassy saw the panic in her eyes. "Get dressed, then just sit still and wait. I'll call you from the co-op." Miss Dallas locked the door behind her.

Sassy wasn't about to sit still. Maybe it wasn't his fault, but Boon was a bad-news boyfriend, and Sassy wasn't about to let him hurt Lula just to show up Daddy. Sassy splashed water on her face from the kitchen faucet, and then raced to her room for her shirt and shoes. If she hurried, she could beat Daddy to the Chisholms'.

Boon's front yard was quiet. Daddy's truck wasn't there yet. Sassy pounded on the door and sucked in the warm, muggy air. Her sides hurt from running the whole way.

The door flew open. She could see the disappointment in the little girl's face. "You're not Mr. Frankie," she said. "Mr. Frankie brings me candy." It was Boon's little sister, but this time there was no baby on her hip.

"Hey, it's me, Sassy. From down the road?" Sassy panted out the words. "Is Boon home?"

"No."

"Charlene! I told you not to answer that door!" Mrs. Chisholm yelled in a voice that was almost harsh. "I don't want to talk to anybody else! Where did you put my cigarettes?"

"It's Sassy from down the road, Mama." The little girl halfway closed the door. Sassy waited. A baby wailed from somewhere inside the house, then Mrs. Chisholm appeared. Her face was puffy and lined, as if she had just woke up from a full sleep.

"Is Boon here?" Sassy asked. "Is he around?"

"Boon's mighty popular this morning," she said.

"I'm looking for my sister, Lula. I thought maybe Boon would know where she was."

"She banged on the door early this morning, but what's that got to do with my boy? He ain't in trouble, is he?"

"Daddy and Miss Dallas are headed over here. Boon and Daddy kind of got into a disagreement yesterday." Sassy could feel her breath coming faster. "Please, Mrs. Chisholm. I got to take Lula home before Daddy finds her here. Is she here?"

"Lula in the family way?" Mrs. Chisholm said. "Damn him. Boon promised me he wouldn't go catting around any more. … I can't have another bawling baby in this house."

Sassy wanted to scream at Mrs. Chisholm to shut up. "Is Lula here?"

One of Boon's little brothers came to the door hugging a Cheerios box with a torn top. "I want some cereal, Mama. I'm hungry."

"I told you that box is empty. Now, get over there and sit down before I take that belt after you!" Mrs. Chisholm yelled. The boy hung on tight to his mother's housecoat. She pushed him away from her and shrugged. "Your sister's been sitting on the back porch since early this morning. I told her Boon left yesterday to look for factory work in Louisville, but she didn't believe—"

Sassy didn't wait for Mrs. Chisholm to finish. Lula looked tiny sitting on the old wood step, like a fragile china doll. The morning sun glinted with the shine of Lula's hair. She was the pretty sister in the family.

"Hey," Sassy said.

Lula looked around, surprised. "Hey."

"You okay?"

"Fine. Just fine." An overnight suitcase sat at Lula's feet.

"You waiting on Boon? Y'all going somewhere?"

"Not exactly." Lula didn't speak for a moment. "I just need to talk to him before I leave town. I know he loved me. ..."

"Boon's not here, Lula. He's gone," Sassy said. "He's a two-timing heartbreaker, and I'll knock every tooth out of his head for you if you want me to."

"I don't want to be without him."

"He ain't worth it."

"He is to me."

"You can't fight Daddy. It's not in you." Sassy was afraid that Lula might break apart like Humpy Dumpty right before her eyes. "Boon'll always be your first love. That's something. *Love Confessions* says you never forget your first love."

The trace of a smile showed in Lula's eyes. "Well, it must be true if it's in *Love Confessions*," she said. Her eyes watered and a loose tear slid down the full length of her cheek.

"Where you going?"

"To California. I'm going to find Mama." Lula's voice broke into a near sob. "I didn't tell you Mama called me. She called me one night."

"When?" Sassy's chest tightened. She didn't want to start crying, too.

"End of May. I didn't know it was her, though. I thought it was some crazy drunk woman. I told her my mama was dead, but she knew our names and everything. It scared me, so I hung up on her. Just hung up."

"Where was she?"

"I don't know." Lula grabbed hold of Sassy's arm. "I didn't know she was Mama. I didn't intend to hang up like that. Do you think I made her mad?" Tears streaked Lula's face.

"Lula, you didn't know. Miss Dallas said Mama might have been real sad when she left us. So sad she didn't know what she was doing. Maybe she's better now."

"I don't know if I can forgive her leaving, Sassy." Lula ran her fingers under her eyes. "But I got to find her. I got to find out."

"Do you know where she is in California?"

"No. ..."

"Lula, she probably ain't even in California now."

"Daddy said that's where she went."

"But she left when I was a baby."

Lula didn't say anything.

"Don't go, Lula." Sassy laid her head on her sister's lap. "I'm sorry about cutting off your hair and smashing up Elvis and every other bad thing I ever did. I ain't been a great sister, but I can't be here without you. Not now. Don't go."

Lula curled her finger around Sassy's hair. "I'm sorry I was so mean. I tried to blame everything on you. I was jealous, I guess, and afraid, too. I didn't want to disappoint Daddy, but ..."

"I know."

"Sassy ..."

"Yeah ..." Sassy turned and looked up at Lula.

"I paid Reeves Hanvey two dollars to kiss you, but not to say those other horrible things, I swear."

"Why did you do that?"

"I don't know." Lula's face was wet with tears now. "I thought maybe he would like you. He was pestering me some ... and I loved Boon but couldn't say anything ... but then Reeves called you Fish Lips and you got mad, and everything got all messed up." Sobs backed up in Lula's voice.

Sassy just let her cry it out. Getting even with Lula felt far away now. Revenge had stirred up plenty of hurt to go around.

Lula sniffed and wiped her nose on the back of her hand. "Reeves and his friends put that fish in your bed. I thought you deserved it after being so mad. … I'm so sorry. It was an awful prank. I don't know what was wrong with me."

Sassy tried to smile. "I'll forgive you if you dry the supper dishes for the rest of the year."

Lula nodded. "Okay." She smiled a small uncertain grin. "I love you, Sassy."

"I love you, too." Sassy sat up. "Do you think Reeves ever kissed a real fish? I mean, how would he know a Fish Lips kiss?"

Lula didn't say anything.

"Maybe we should start that rumor when school starts." Sassy laughed thinking about it.

Lula closed her eyes. "Has Daddy said anything to you?" she said, almost mournful. "I can't stay here if he hates us. If he thinks we'll run around and hurt him … I'm not like Mama. … I'm not."

"Miss Dallas says he still loves us—says we're his whole life. Daddy's just real angry, but he'll come around. Everything's going to get better."

Lula broke down and sobbed into her hands. "What are we going to do if Mama comes back?" she said through her tears. "What are we going to say to her?"

"I don't know. We'll just have to figure it out. We'll have to plan out something special to say." Sassy's heart seemed to fill up every open space in her chest. "We can practice on it together if you come back home, Lula. Please. I need you. I need my sister."

Just then, Daddy's truck turned into the yard. He barely had the engine shut down when he raced to Lula and Sassy and pulled them into his arms. Sassy held on to Daddy and Lula with everything she had, even when they walked back to the truck tripping all over each other.

Miss Dallas waited. She took Lula's suitcase and hugged the girls, then hugged Daddy, and hugged the girls again. They huddled close into the truck, and Sassy slipped her hand into Lula's and grinned at her sister. Daddy turned the key and the engine fired up, then he held Lula's other hand and nobody spoke. Daddy and Lula and Sassy and Miss Dallas didn't need any words just then.

As they drove out of the yard, Sassy watched the Chisholm kids gawk at them from the front porch as if they had just seen Santa Claus. But Sassy knew it was love they had witnessed. Real-life love. And it was not one bit like *Love Confessions*. That's all Sassy needed to know.